BACK IN THE DAY

BAY AREA BLUES

KATRINA JACKSON

SEA PORT PRESS LLC

CONTENT WARNINGS

Parental death
Grief
Recreational drug use

This past June, thousands of people streamed into the Monterey fairgrounds, just on the right side of the railroad tracks in the small oceanfront town, ready to experience a musical revelation.

While the fairgrounds were too far away to see the Pacific, you could feel the water in the rhythmic waves as one band crashed into another from all over the musical spectrum.

The sun was relentless, immediately bleaching out each performance in our minds before the final chords had faded into that distant sound of the ocean.

The crowd was as eclectic as the lineup. For some people, the festival was just a pitstop on the way to yet another show; people constantly chasing the euphoric high you can only experience in the wailing cry of an electric guitar. And for others, the Monterey Pop Festival was the highlight of their year. A break from the monotony of their mundane lives. It was the kind of experience that gave each person who experienced it something different — something new — and won't be so easily forgotten. What we experienced in Monterey will stick with us if we let it.

If you were there, I promise you one day someone will ask you to think about moments that changed your life. Moments that blanketed you in the good vibrations of the best music, the sun beating down on your forehead, and that sure moment when you had the opportunity to make a real connection with another person, and you took it. Moments that offered you the chance to take the first step into becoming whoever you think you were meant to be.

And for so many of us, that moment occurred at the Monterey Fairgrounds.

"The Monterey Pop Festival: Music and Magic on an Unforgettable Weekend"
by Alonzo Reid
Staff Reporter
Village Voice, August 1967

2010

"HEY, POP. POP." Amir sat back on his haunches and turned to look toward the bedroom door behind him. He waited a few seconds, listening to the silence. The muffled sound of music from across the hall had been like white noise while he'd been working. Now he strained his ears, waiting to hear some sign of life from the other bedroom. "Dad," he called again, louder this time.

"Boy, if you don't stop yelling in my house!" Amir's father, Alonzo, yelled back. As usual, he didn't see any contradiction in yelling at him about not yelling. Amir knew trying to point out the contradiction wouldn't get him anywhere but a replay of the same lecture he'd been hearing for nearly all his life that ended with, "Do as I say, not as I do," and he didn't have the energy or time for that.

He stood and brushed the thin layer of dust from his hands, the particles seeming almost beautiful in the light streaming in through the window. He had to pick his way through the half-packed boxes littering the floor in the room that had been his mother's studio, a guest bedroom, his father's office, and a nursery for a cousin's daughter for a few months while his cousin was getting on her feet in Amir's lifetime. Often, it had been two or more of those things at once. In recent years, it had become the dumping ground for the memorabilia of their past — Amir and his sister's trophies, his mom's spare cameras, old floppy disks with drafts of his dad's work — all the things they wanted to save, but not sure yet for whom.

When Amir stepped into the hall, he could hear the music much more clearly, although it still sounded staticky because Alonzo was playing it on a radio that was probably older than Amir. It was tuned to KBLX, the only station his father recognized these days; the only station that played *real* music, Alonzo sometimes said with a laugh, not so much as a judgment but just a professional observation.

But even through that ancient speaker, the plucking sound of an electric guitar cut through the distortion and filled the hallway, loud and melodic, as if even the ancient technology couldn't stop a hit from hitting.

Love'll make you do right...

The music grew louder as Alonzo turned the volume up, always ready to help a great song shine.

There was a smile on Amir's face as he moved across the hall. "We playin' Reverend Al?" Amir called down the hallway. "Is that the mood today?"

"Mmmhmm," his father hummed, maybe in answer or maybe just in tune.

Amir walked the last few steps and stopped in the doorway of his parents' bedroom. He leaned against the doorjamb, looking into a room that hadn't changed in as long as he could remember, not in significant ways, at least. He hovered just over the threshold, as he so often did. He used to reach inside the room for a glass in his mother's hand and then run downstairs to fill it with water so she could take her hypertension medication before bed. Sometimes, he'd stand on this threshold craning his neck to read over his dad's shoulder as the older man's eyes scanned over a sheaf of type-written pages, a ballpoint pen behind his ear, and a pencil between his lips.

But in the five years since his mother's death, Amir felt as if he was in this room more times than ever before. Helping Alonzo pack up his mother's clothing when he was ready, going through the medication on Alonzo's bedside table to make sure the prescriptions were up to date and filled. Or on those few days in the past couple of years when he'd had to sit at his father's bedside, listening to his raspy, even breaths, grasping for a sense of calm in the reminder that he was here.

His father was still here.

The last five years of reminders that he had one parent

left were bittersweet. There would never be enough time, he knew now. There hadn't been enough time with his mother, and one day, no matter how much longer Alonzo lived, Amir knew that he would confront the premature loss, and he wouldn't be ready.

There was also the pain of seeing his father, as he was in this moment, in an unnatural state. That's what Alonzo called it — as if every day without his late wife was some alternate reality he was desperately trying to escape. Hell, knowing Alonzo, maybe it was. He accepted Ada's death only because he planned to follow her as soon as possible, as soon as nature would allow. And in the meantime, he went about life with the mission to preserve his wife's memory. He lived each day as a reminder that he had walked through the world with someone else and every day without her hurt.

Amir looked around at the room that had become a shrine. Alonzo still slept on his side of the bed. While they'd donated most of his mom's clothes to the shelter at their church, Second Temple Baptist, her half of the closet was still full of pieces Alonzo hadn't been ready to let go of just yet. Her Bible and a family picture from sometime around Amir's sixth birthday were still arranged neatly on his mother's bedside table. Her reading glasses used to complete that tableau, but a few years ago, Alonzo had donated them during a drive at his optometrist's office to provide lenses for homeless people. It had taken him weeks to make the decision to give those glasses up, but he'd rationalized it as he so often did these days.

"*Your mama woulda liked that,*" he'd said with tears in his eyes on the drive to the optometrist. The weight of Alonzo's grief seemed to slow time, stretching out every day, every hour, so Alonzo could inspect these moments without his wife in excruciating detail.

Everyone worried that Alonzo wasn't moving past his grief, but Amir knew for a fact that he wasn't. How could he? Who could move past a loss that great?

Sometimes, Amir walked into his parents' house, and his mother's presence was so strong that for a few minutes, he let himself believe that she was just about to push through the front door, her arms full of Safeway bags or humming a hymn the church choir had been practicing or even with her friend Deidre who lived down the street hot on her heels. *Used* to live down the street, he had to remind himself more than once. Deidre died last year. Sometimes, he walked into a room in this house, and he thought he could almost hear the faint echoes of his mother's laughter from another room, upstairs, outside, always just at the edge of his vision.

How Alonzo lived with the ghost of her was incomprehensible, but he did, and Amir's terrified obsession was that living in that grief was leeching all the energy he had left. He worried that whatever time he had left with his father was slipping away faster than it should, spurred on by Alonzo's desire to be reunited with his wife.

Amir's eyes moved around the room before settling on his father's back. Alonzo was sitting at the foot of the bed with his head bent over a box at his feet. To Amir's eyes, Alonzo Reid looked just a bit smaller, thinner, and stooped each time he saw him. He couldn't be certain if his perception was reality or just a manifestation of his fear and impending grief.

Probably both. Either way, there was an ache in Amir's chest that refused to go away.

Alonzo was Amir's role model. To his child eyes, no one on television or in his books could compare to his father. When Amir was a boy, Alonzo had seemed larger than life, and not just because he was nearly six-foot-five with big hands that felt heavy and reassuring on Amir's shoulders. Or because Alonzo had the kind of laugh that boomed through the house, and his wife used to fuss at him about waking the kids. He sometimes did, but his apologies were always just as loud. And not because Alonzo could make anything out of wood. Or the fact that he was a great dancer but a terrible singer. And definitely not because Alonzo used to serenade his wife in the softest terrible voice that made her laugh and smile and cringe with nothing but love in her eyes.

It was all of those things and more. Alonzo was Amir's blueprint. Hero worship wasn't a strong enough phrase to describe the way Amir felt about his father. And sadness wasn't a strong enough emotion for what he felt having to watch his hero waste away. Losing his wife dragged

Alonzo out of the realm of the fantastic into reality. It made Alonzo mortal. And it made Amir's world seem more dangerous and darker each day.

"Hey, pop," Amir said in a gentle voice, trying to hide the well of emotion swelling in his breast.

"Mmmhmm?" his father hummed again, the question clear in the light lifting of his voice and the tilt of his head in the direction of his son. But he kept his gaze on the box in front of him.

"What do you wanna do with that box of dolls?"

That made Alonzo freeze for a second before he turned slowly toward the door, his eyebrows lifted in confusion. "Box of dolls?"

"Yeah, those creepy porcelain ones in those weird dresses."

It took a few seconds for his father's face to lift from confusion into understanding. When it did, his jack-hammer of a laugh made Amir's heart jump in surprise. It didn't boom as loud as Amir remembered, but it rumbled through his chest and seemed to harmonize with Reverend Al, deep and crackly just the same. "Those are for your sister. Your mama said so."

"Does Amaya know that?" Amir knew for a fact that Amaya did not know that, and she would object fiercely. She hated those dolls. They used to sit on a shelf above her bed. Amaya said they sometimes kept her up at night. She thought they were cursed.

There was an earthquake the year she turned twelve,

nothing major, barely even noticeable. But in a stroke of pre-teen genius, Amaya had taken the opportunity to knock a few of those scary ass dolls from off that shelf. Their mom had been devastated, cradling the fragile dolls with smashed faces carefully in her hands. Their dad had immediately gotten his tool belt and begun dismantling the shelf, grumbling about it being a safety hazard, even though he'd put it up himself and it had been quite secure.

Amaya said that first night of sleep without those creepy dolls was the best of her young life.

Alonzo's shoulders shook with a gentle chuckle. "I suspect she's been hoping they all broke by now, but they're hers nonetheless." He locked eyes with Amir, his smile flattening into seriousness. "Tell her she can get rid of them when I'm gone but not before. Your mama had me driving all over town to find those damn dolls when she was pregnant with her. Mahogany Misses."

"Mahogany what?"

"Mahogany Misses," his father repeated a little bit louder. "That's what they're called. Soon as your mother found out we were havin' a girl, the first thing she said was that she wanted those little porcelain dolls but in brown."

"That sounds like mama," Amir chuckled.

His father nodded slowly. His eyes shifted just to the left and grew glassy with tears — an uncomfortably common occurrence these days. Alonzo moved a shaking hand to his face to wipe those tears away, still nodding wistfully.

"I'll tell Maya," Amir said softly. "You need any help in here?"

"Nah, I think I got it," his father said, turning back to the box between his feet.

Amir looked around the room, surprised to see the number of boxes with actual things inside them. This move had been a long time coming, this inevitable moment coming at a snail's pace. It hadn't been easy, but Amir had thought it would be harder.

Almost as soon as their mother had passed, Amir and his older sister Amaya had begun to worry about their father living in the two-story four-bedroom house alone. Their grief counselor had reassured them that these were normal fears but advised against rushing themselves or their father into any big changes. They hadn't taken his advice and tried to get Alonzo to leave the house a few months after their mother's death. That had been a mistake. Their counselor hadn't told them, "I told you so," but they'd felt that energy and backed off. Besides, grief aside, Alonzo had lived on his own remarkably well.

But in the last few years, so much seemed to change and quickly.

Alonzo's eyesight had started to deteriorate a couple of years ago, and it took a few scary months to convince him to relinquish his license. He had a phantom pain in his hip that sometimes made it near-impossible to get out of bed without help. He was opposed to a home health aide, so Amir and Amaya and a few of their play cousins had created a complex phone tree of people who could be called on to help him on his bad days.

But Alonzo's hearing was still perfect, and on his good days, he got out of bed on his own, showered, dressed, and spent the entire day in the darkened living room listening to the entire catalogue of his favorite musicians in bliss. His good days still put Amir on edge. He barely spoke and only ate if someone put his meals on the tv tray in front of him. If left to his own devices, Alonzo would sit there, nodding his head, tapping his feet, and singing along when a lyric moved him somewhere deep in his soul.

Time meant nothing to Alonzo on those days, only the mood and the music. Only the memory of his wife. That was no way to live.

After nearly two years of whispered discussions at family get-togethers and nervous phone calls between the siblings, Amir and Amaya finally approached their father again about living on his own. They'd been prepared for a knockdown, drag-out fight and had gotten a sad, slow nod of agreement. Alonzo agreed to move on two conditions: he asked for a few months to pack up his and his late wife's belongings himself — with his children's intermittent help — and he made them promise not to sell the house. Amir and Amaya had agreed immediately because they were terrified that he might change his mind, but also because the thought of someone who wasn't them sifting through their mother's books, deciding what to give away or keep made their skin itch. What if someone accidentally threw away her good Bundt cake pan? Selling the house was just as incomprehensible. This house was their legacy. Their parents had begun to save for a home before children were even a thought in their heads. This house was a permanent thing they could give their future children, a permanent thing neither of them had ever known.

After that, things went smoothly. Even the decision about where to move Alonzo was easy. Amaya lived in a converted warehouse artist's commune in San Francisco. She shared a large room with her girlfriend that also served as their art studio. Alonzo loved to visit on occasion to watch his daughter paint, but living there wasn't an option. So, Amir began to clear out the spare bedroom in his condo, and they got to work collecting boxes for Alonzo to fill at his leisure.

But Amir was a pessimist, and he was always prepared for things to go wrong. No matter how smooth this move had been going, it wasn't over yet. For months, he'd lived with the fear that they were just one dusty tchotchke away from the whole arrangement falling apart. It was one thing for Alonzo to pack everything up, but it was an entirely different thing for him to leave the house where his wife had baked her famous pineapple upside-down cakes for every one of his birthdays and soothed her crying babies with lullaby versions of Tina Turner's greatest hits for Amaya and a Motown medley for Amir. Where she had danced around the living room with Alonzo to Barry

White's greatest hits. Where she had taken her last breaths.

The finality of what was to come was terrifyingly sad to Amir, and he couldn't imagine how his father was handling it all so well. So Amir was prepared for the mood to change and quickly.

"After lunch, we gotta tackle them records," Alonzo said, pushing the box between his feet away.

Amir could see now that it was full of his mother's science fiction paperbacks, a worn copy of Octavia Butler's *Kindred* on top. He smiled. "You finally ready to go through them?"

Alonzo shook his head. "Ain't nothing to go through. Just gotta wipe 'em down and pack 'em up."

"Pops, we can't—"

His father turned to him with raised eyebrows, and Amir pressed his lips shut quickly.

He wanted to make this easy on him. He wanted to tiptoe around all the hard things, but he couldn't.

They'd done all the easy stuff first. They donated most of the dishes to the church. Amaya took her mother's cast iron skillet, casserole dish, the bakeware, and a spatula that apparently meant something to three, now four genera- tions of their mother's family. Their father kept his moth- er's good jewelry in a nondescript box in the closet. They'd already had the conversation about what would happen to those modest pieces when he died. Amaya had claimed their mother's diamond earrings and necklace, Amir wanted his mother's engagement ring, and they would split their wedding bands. But they couldn't avoid the hard stuff anymore. Apparently, Alonzo was willing to go along to get along, except when it came to the hundreds of vinyl records neatly organized and displayed in their living room.

Amir's parents had loved music, and the evidence of that was all over their house — framed posters from concerts they'd attended through the years, band t-shirts Amir and Amaya had inherited in their teenage years, threadbare and worn-in, the kind of soft to the touch that could only be achieved by hand-washing and drying in the sun over too many years. Music was everywhere in Amir's memories, a soundtrack to his life that was all the hits, plus the deep cuts and a live performance that no one remembered but the four people who had made this house a home.

There was Earth, Wind & Fire at the first summer cookout every year. Nat King Cole and every soul and blues holiday album around the winter holidays. The sounds of Patrice Rushen and Minnie Riperton late at night and an image of his parents dancing chest-to-chest, arms wrapped tight around one another in the middle of the living room, undercut with the sound of his and Amaya's secret giggles. There was Aretha on Saturday mornings and the smell of bleach. And at the center of it all was the most epic record collection Amir had ever seen outside of a record store.

Their living room was half a hexagon, the only remainder of the Victorian house that had stood in this lot from back when no Black people lived in Oakland. Apparently, the first thing Alonzo had done when they moved in was build an entire built-in system to hold their records, adding to it one boxy unit at a time as their collection grew right along with their kids.

Right along with their love.

Their records were organized alphabetically by band name and then chronologically by year. The low boxes created a bench, with the family's record player unit sat at the center of the collection where other people might keep a television; but this house was built on music. It had seeped into the paint, the plaster, and down into the foundation. Music was the glue holding the structure up and strengthening the bonds of their family.

But Amir didn't have room in his condo for a collection that large.

"Pop, can't you just choose your favorites, and we can box the rest up for storage?"

"Hell nah. Besides, they're all my favorites. I don't choose between you and Maya, so I'm not about to choose between my other babies."

Amir rolled his eyes. "You know I don't have that kind of room in my condo, dad."

"I tried to tell you not to buy that place."

"It's brand-new."

"And in the middle of nowhere. Anyway, you don't

have room *now*, but once I'm settled, you and me are gonna make some shelves like I got downstairs. I made those, you know?"

"I know, dad."

"Don't they look good?"

"They look fine. I just don't get it..."

"Get what? Good music?" He sighed and shook his head. "Where'd we fail you?" he muttered to himself before turning to his son and winking slyly.

It had the same effect it always did, and Amir smiled. "I just wanna understand, pops. I'll pack 'em up and move 'em into my small ass condo if you want."

"Watch your mouth."

"Sorry. I'll do it. I just want to understand why you need to have them *all* with you."

Now that he'd said what he needed to say, Amir pressed his lips shut, breathing heavily through his nose. Talking back to his father wasn't any easier just because he was grown. He stood there, watching his father watch him. His dark brown face was deep with wrinkles around his mouth and between his eyes, not because of age but because of a life well-lived. That's what Amir's mother used to say about wrinkles; they were a sign of a life lived, and she'd attributed so many of hers to her husband.

"*See that wrinkle?*" she used to ask, pointing at a groove around her mouth. "*I got that from your daddy and all his corny knock-knock jokes. What's the benefit of getting old if you can't see it on your face or feel it in your limbs?"*

Finally, Alonzo was done considering him, and he spoke. "I ever tell you how I met your mama?" he asked out of the blue.

"A concert," Amir said with a soft sigh.

"Yeah, but did I ever tell you about that concert? *The* concert?"

"What's that mean? *The concert?*"

Alonzo stood stiffly from the bed. Amir tried not to squint critically, but his heart was racing as he braced himself for any sign that his father was in pain.

"Tell you what, how 'bout you order some barbecue from JJ's for lunch, and I'll go through the whole story, track by track?"

"Pop, JJ's closed two years ago. Remember?"

His father's face fell. "Damn, I forgot about that. Best fucking barbecue in the city."

"Watch your mouth," Amir said.

His father sucked his teeth, but the smile returned to his face. "What about Mama Rae's? They still open?" he asked sarcastically because he knew the answer to this question.

Amir smiled back. "Yes, sir. You know they don't deliver, though. I can go pick something up."

His father brushed the air. "Nah, let's take a break. Get a good meal. You know Martha taught your mama how to cook those red beans and rice you always liked?"

"She did?"

"Yeah, I'll tell you that story too."

"You want me to make a list?" Amir teased.

"Probably should. Lord knows I won't remember."

"Alright, old man. Let's go. I'll buy you lunch, and then we'll get back to packing. Sound good?"

His father nodded. "I 'specially like the part where you're paying. You know how expensive you were to raise?"

Amir backed into the hallway with another hard sigh that turned into a chuckle, and in the dark, quiet hallway, it sounded almost like his mother's.

1967

ALONZO WAS GOING to be late.

He'd gotten a phone call from the senior arts editor at the *Village Voice*, Ed Gallegos, at just past eight o'clock last night. They needed him to step in and cover the Monterey Pop Festival if he was interested.

If. He. Was. Interested.

He'd been a third-string freelancer at a bunch of papers all over the Bay Area for nearly three years. Hell, he'd even filed a few articles in Los Angeles because he had a friend looking to bring on some new reviewers. But the *Voice* was the paper that mattered. The *Voice* was the paper where he had pinned all his hopes and dreams about becoming a real journalist one day, not just stringing a few assignments together when and where he could, making ends meet picking up handyman jobs around the neighborhood. Getting by any way he could.

He tried to stay ready, but there was ready, and there was 'clear your weekend and get down to Monterey on less than twelve hours' notice' ready, and Alonzo was not the latter. Hell, he didn't even have a car. He'd spent most of last night trying to track down his best friend and room-mate Toonie at one of his many girlfriends' houses to see if he could borrow his car or get a ride at least.

He'd been seriously considering hitch-hiking south when Toonie had come back to their apartment with a new girlfriend Alonzo had never met on his arm. He'd handed over the keys to his Nova with half a tank of gas and a deep nod for luck. Alonzo drove as fast as he dared, but still, he was going to be late. Not late enough to miss the first set of the festival, but late to meet the freelance photographer Ed said would be waiting just inside the fair-ground's gates for him.

By the time he pulled Toonie's car into the parking lot, he was two hours late and sweating.

Alonzo had never been to Monterey County Fair-grounds before, not when he was a broke kid and not now that he was a broke man. This was one of the things he liked about being a journalist, the ability to experience something new, something denied him. It was a perk that had an economic value but emotionally was impossible to quantify.

In another life, Alonzo would have been a dreamer, but in this life, he didn't have that luxury.

He'd been working nearly half his life already. He

used to hang outside the pool halls in West Oakland. At first, that loitering was practical. He'd waited on the curb for his father to get ejected from the front door, drunk and belligerent, so he could help him stumble home. After a while, he started running errands for the hardcore gamblers to make a little pocket change. But while he was waiting for a new assignment, he used to sit on the same curb where he'd helped his father up from the ground, with a notebook and a pen because writing was the job of his dreams. And writing about music was what Alonzo sometimes thought heaven on earth might be like.

There was something about the way he felt at a show, his slim pad of paper in his back pocket, a pen tucked into his afro, maybe a bottle of beer long gone warm in his other hand, someone wailing on an electric guitar on stage with expert, nimble fingers, each note making his skin feel like a trembling earthquake was building up to tear him down from the inside out. Music was not practical. Music stirred the soul. Becoming a music journalist was the only time Alonzo allowed himself to dream about something that was anything but practical.

All his life, he'd been holding this unfathomable fantasy all to himself, and on the drive to Monterey, he could feel that this concert was the key to making it come true. All he had to do was write the best review of his life and hope the photographer didn't hate him enough to accidentally forget to take the cap off his lens.

"Fuck," he groaned under his breath, pulling into the first empty parking spot he passed.

He didn't even take a moment to compose himself after the long drive. He'd had to stop by the local *Voice* office to pick up the envelope with his press pass and tickets and a little bit of money for incidentals. His quick perusal of those bills indicated that it might be enough to cover some lean meals and some of his gas at best, but he didn't have time to worry about that.

He threw the lanyard with his pass over his head and placed his ticket and a little bit of the little bit of money into his fanny pack, which already held his small notebook, a few pens, and his wallet. He locked Toonie's car, shoved the keys to the bottom of his bag, and threw it over his neck for the jog to the fairground front gates. The sun was uncomfortably high in the sky, and small ponds of sweat began to form on his forehead and at his lower back, making an already uncomfortable situation worse.

There was a small line to get into the fairgrounds, and Alonzo went to the one that seemed to be moving faster than the others, but he kept his eyes roving, ready to move to another line if necessary; anything to get inside as fast as possible. He held up his press pass to the lady running the turnstile, and she frowned at him until he remembered to hand over his ticket. He snatched his stub from her fingers and rushed inside.

Ed had said the photographer would meet him just inside the turnstiles, and maybe if he'd been less tired after a full day helping Tommy Lucas move his grandmother into a new apartment or less excited about the last-minute assignment, he would have remembered to ask some crucial questions such as: What's the photographer look like? What's his name? What'll he be wearing? But hindsight was 20/20, and foolishness was eternal, so as soon as he made it into the fairgrounds, he looked frantically around for anyone with a camera. Unfortunately, there were lots of people with cameras clutched in their hands or slung over their necks, and Alonzo couldn't stop the self-recrimination from washing over him in waves.

The sun felt as if it was sitting on the back of his neck. He grabbed the front of his t-shirt and started pulling at it, hoping he could cool off while scanning the grounds for the photographer. Assuming the man hadn't left nearly two hours ago, Alonzo hoped he wasn't a sweaty mess when they linked up. He unzipped his fanny pack and pulled out a dark blue bandana he kept there, using it to mop at his damp forehead, and then tied it around his head. He checked his watch and swore to himself. Knowing his luck, the photographer was long gone, and there wasn't anyone Alonzo could blame but himself.

Just a few hours ago, he'd felt as if this concert — this moment — was his chance, but now that feeling was evaporating in the dry summer heat.

"You look hot," someone said from behind him.

Alonzo whirled around and came face-to-face — well, face to just about her forehead — with a woman who made him blink a few too many times as he tried to make sure he was seeing what he thought he was seeing.

"You don't look so bad yourself," he breathed, a lopsided grin on his face.

She eyed him up and down and back up again with a frown tilting her mouth. "Boy, you wish." She crossed her arms in front of her chest. "I mean, you look like you're melting, your hair's flat on one side, and you're late. What made you wear all those clothes anyway?" she asked, each word dripping with as much disdain as sweat on his back.

"You sayin' I should be wearing less?" Alonzo asked and then cringed. If Toonie was here, he'd have walked away in disgust. Alonzo had never been good at flirting, but this was his worst effort by far. It had barely started, and he knew he'd be embarrassed about this for a decade at least.

She rolled her eyes before turning to look at the crowd streaming into the fairgrounds. Alonzo followed her line of sight, and it took a second to catch her meaning. Truth be told, there were about as many people dressed in a pair of jeans and a t-shirt like him, but he saw just as many people in shorts and tanks, dresses, and even less, which only seemed to make his shirt stick even more firmly to his skin, and he sighed.

"I got dressed in a hurry," he said in a poor effort to defend himself.

He gave her the same sort of once-over she'd given him, and unlike her, he had no complaints at what he saw. She was wearing a yellow floral sundress. The thin straps bared smooth deep brown shoulders. The hem hit just about mid-thigh, exposing a pair of legs that were an even darker brown and looked thick enough to— "I'm not here for the concert," he blurted out before he let himself continue that line of thought. He lifted his eyes immediately to her face and found her watching him with a graceful smirk twisting her glossy lips. Alonzo couldn't help but sigh once more at his pitiful circumstances. "I mean, I'm here to work," he said quietly.

"You planning to keep to the shade?"

He put his hands on his hips and glared down at her for a few seconds before he was forced to focus his gaze on the rounded tip of her nose. It seemed like the safest place to look but made it difficult to fully commit to the glare. Eventually, he just gave up and threw his arms to either side of his body as the only response he could offer to her very reasonable question.

And that made her laugh.

She uncrossed her arms and pressed her palms to her chest. Her eyes closed, and her lush mouth spread on a bark of surprise followed by the most delicate peal of laughter, and it was the most beautiful chime Alonzo had ever heard outside of the breakdown in a love song. She laughed with her entire body, every muscle in her face lifted, and her fingertips had curled gently into her skin, the cracked light blue nail polish only adding to her charm. The fact that she was not in any way trying to charm him only seemed to sweep him up in this moment even more forcefully.

She laughed at him hard enough to bring tears to her eyes, and all he could do was grin and bear the desire curling in his gut. It was a good thing Toonie weren't here. He would have shaken his head and called him pitiful, and he would have been damn right.

After an uncomfortably long period of time, she wiped at her wet eyes and shook her head. "Well, you best be careful. Walking around in all this sun covered up like that, you'll probably faint."

"I'm not gonna faint," he said, rolling his eyes.

"And I'm telling you right now that carrying you to the shade is *not* in my job description."

"Why would you—"

"I told Ed that I'm just here to take pictures, groove to some music, and get paid."

It took a few seconds for that sentence to sink in. "*You're* the photographer?" he exclaimed.

Her eyebrows lifted. "I am. Do we have a problem?"

"N-no. No. I just... You're just not what I was expecting."

She crossed her arms and frowned up at him. "And what exactly were you expecting?"

"Someone ugly," he said immediately. "Who smelled like cigarette smoke and stale beer."

She slowly dropped her arms, and that frown lifted,

not into a smile but flattened into a forced crush of her lips together as she tried not to smile.

But Alonzo wanted her to laugh, so he kept going. "Maybe wearing a Hawaiian shirt with long, dirty hair."

"Stop," she mumbled, barely moving her lips, trying to contain her laughter.

"Maybe dirty fingernails and bare feet?"

That broke her, and this time, when she doubled over in laughter, Alonzo let himself smile along with her. All his senses drank her in; that laugh, the sight of her shoulders shaking, and the way each new, moisturized depth of her hair caught new rays of sunlight.

"So you've met Stevie, huh?" she asked in breathy laughter.

Alonzo ducked his head. "He seemed nice, but..."

"But even he'll tell you that he's not too concerned about human contact. He's a nature photographer most of the time."

"Oh, yeah?"

She nodded. "Mmmhmm. He sells his work at a few galleries in San Francisco. You should check 'em out some time."

"Maybe we should go together."

"I don't shit where I eat," she said simply, shocking the tentative smile from Alonzo's face.

"I— I didn't mean—"

"Yes. You did. But I'm not going to hold that against you. I'm just letting you know upfront that you should treat me like you'd treat Stevie. This is my job. Now I don't know about you, but my landlord don't take IOUs when I'm short, and fucking around with someone I work with is a great way to always come up short. So...you ready?"

Alonzo's mouth had gone dry. "I'm sorry," he said, once he unstuck his tongue from the roof of his mouth.

"Don't be sorry, just be professional," she said with a shrug that, even in its nonchalance, Alonzo realized was anything but casual.

He nodded quickly. "Yes, ma'am," he said.

That made her smile again.

"How did you know I was me?" he asked.

"Ed said you was green, lanky, and dark-skinned with a good smile."

"Ed said I had a good smile?"

She tipped her head to the left toward the fairgrounds just as the harsh chord of someone's guitar warm-up screeched into the air. "Come on. Let's get to work."

She didn't answer his question, and he watched her walk away from him with a bewildered smile. He kept his eyes on her shoulders even though he wanted to see her ass in that dress or, hell, even the backs of her thighs. But he hadn't looked at Stevie that way, so he refused to let his eyes move any lower.

But then she turned to look over her right shoulder with a quirked eyebrow and a wry grin. Their gazes crashed into one another. "We'll buy you a new shirt on the way," she called.

He frowned but moved to follow.

"And my name's Ada, by the way."

Unfortunately, he loved her name and the slight Southern accent in the way she said it. "Alonzo," he called, moving just a little bit faster to catch up.

"What?" she yelled before turning around and walking backward. Her smile was beautiful; big, bright, and mocking, a combination that shouldn't have worked on him except it did. It worked so well that he was mad about it — because Ada with the lush fro and the pillowy soft lips and the no-nonsense frown was the exact kind of woman he conjured in his mind when Toonie asked him why he was always working. Why he *never* seemed to date.

Because he'd never met Ada before, apparently.

He had to jog a few steps before he met up with her. She turned, and they fell into an easy stride together. "My name's Alonzo. Alonzo Reid," he said, wiping his hand on his pants before offering it to her.

She looked him up and down again with a smirking scrutiny that he liked just a little too much to hide, so he smiled eagerly in return.

She stuck her hand out and grasped his in a warm, thankfully dry grip. "Ada Carr," she said softly.

"Nice to meet you, Ada Carr."

"I'll reserve my judgment, Alonzo Reid."

"AND I KNEW in that moment that I was gon' marry her," Alonzo told Amir with watery eyes and a gentle grin that turned into a soft chuckle. "It took her a little longer to realize she felt the same way 'bout me, mind you. But that was alright with me. She was always gonna be worth the wait."

2010

THE DRIVE to Mama Rae's Kitchen was short only because the route from his parents' house to the restaurant was one of the most familiar in Amir's life.

Nestled in a part of East Oakland the news media used to describe as "rough," Mama Rae's was an institution in Black Oakland before there were enough Black people in Oakland to count on the census. Amir had composed a well-researched but terribly written essay about it when he was in high school. Even though the neighborhood had changed drastically in over half a century, Mama Rae's Kitchen and a dive bar with a terrible liquor selection but a pristine jukebox called Tommie B's were a time capsule of Oakland in those first few years after the Second World War. They were the lone reminders that once upon a time, this community used to be *something beautiful*. That's at least what his parents used to say when they'd describe the Oakland of their youth.

Still, Mama Rae's was like hallowed ground for his family and so many others all around the city. It was the place they came for good Texas barbecue. The place that made cobbler just like someone's mama or grandmama or... someone special but long gone. It was the place where people met up before a city-wide march. The place everyone could count on to be there, even when everything seemed to always be changing until it was gone.

Every time he stepped into Mama Rae's, he'd suddenly remember that the restaurant had opened in 1939. It wasn't even really a restaurant, just a kitchen the original owner, Evelyn, rented out a few days a week in someone's boardinghouse near the docks. She'd cooked Southern food for wartime migrants and made enough to finally open a brick-and-mortar establishment in 1950 and named it after her mother, whose own restaurant had been burned down in Galveston when local police discovered that all but two of her children had left town in the dead of the night. This restaurant allowed her to pay homage to a mother she sometimes worried she'd never see again because getting the fuck out of Texas had been serious and perilous business in those days but returning was still very much an unknown.

Mama Rae's was the site of so many of Amir's childhood memories that it was almost as sacred as the home he was helping pack up right now. Going to Rae's Kitchen was somehow a normal fact of life and also a treat. It was where they went when Ada didn't want to cook but had a craving for shrimp and grits, a thing Alonzo could never make to her specific tastes. To be fair, she couldn't make it to her tastes either, but Amir noted that it was a failing that only Alonzo seemed to take as such. They went to Rae's to pick up a pan of cobbler for their Fourth of July barbecues. While they waited to pick up their order, Ada would send Amir to the Muslim bakery next door to pick up a couple of bean pies.

Mama Rae's catered his mother's repast, although he couldn't remember who'd called in that order. Maybe no one had. Maybe Lena, the current owner, had started working on a menu the day she found out that Ada had passed. Either way, his mother would have approved, and so much of the way they'd all lived their lives had been to bask in the bountiful light of Ada Carr Reid's approval.

Especially Alonzo.

Amir opened the glass front door and waited patiently as Alonzo walked slowly and carefully inside. The vinegary scent of greens and barbecue sauce hit Amir's nose immediately, and it pulled an unexpected, involuntary smile across his mouth as a soft rumble of hunger burned through his gut. The sound of forks and spoons scraping ceramic plates was almost deafening, but of course, Alonzo didn't hear any of that because the first thing Alonzo noticed when he entered a room was Ada. The second was the music.

He sucked his teeth in annoyance and shook his head. "Now, what's this shit?"

"Pop," Amir mumbled. "Be nice."

"The hell I will. Martha would be rolling over in her grave if she heard this. When she was alive, the only time the dial left KBLX was on Sundays. Martha ain't have no time for God, but we ain't hold that against her." Alonzo leaned toward him and whispered that last sentence as if it was a secret that Martha was an atheist — the first atheist Amir had ever met and the funniest woman in all of East Oakland as far as he was concerned. But *everybody* knew Martha didn't go to church, just like they knew Martha would have a fresh pot of grits on the stove waiting for whenever church let out.

"Two?" The young woman who appeared in front of them looked as uncomfortable as everyone did in Mama Rae's honey gold and brown uniform shirts and black pants. Something about that discomfort made everyone look the same and so vaguely familiar.

"Is that Kayla?" Alonzo rasped.

The young girl's face lit up. "Hi, Mr. Reid. How are you?"

"I'm old. How are you? How's your daddy?"

"We're all good. My dad was just talking about you yesterday, actually."

Alonzo put his hands on his hips and frowned at her. "Why? What he mess up now?"

She slapped a hand over her mouth to hide her giggles.

She looked all of fourteen, and it reminded Amir of the summer he spent messing up everyone's orders when he worked at Mama Rae's. Martha was still alive then but getting softer in her old age, so she'd sent her daughter Lena to fire him after barely a month.

Kayla was still laughing when she answered Alonzo's question. "He's been teaching me how to play the guitar. He said you taught him?"

"Sure did," Alonzo said and then turned to Amir with a megawatt smile on his face. "Her daddy was one of my first students when I used to teach music at Mac."

"Oh, yeah?"

"Mmmhmm, Kayvon Miller. He was in your mama's photography class too. One of her best students, she used to say. Tell him I saw one of his pictures at that gallery in Berkeley. You know, the one that won't ever give a Black artist a show but loves to put our work in the window, so no one protests out front."

Kayla rolled her eyes and nodded. "Dad calls them Fake Ass Fredericks."

"Fredericks Gallery. Yeah, that's their name. Anyway, you tell your dad I see him, alright."

Her face was beaming as she nodded. "Yes, sir. Do you want a booth, or do you want to sit by the window?"

Alonzo deferred to Amir as he always did.

"Booth, please," he said.

And again, as he always did, Alonzo nodded and hummed as if this decision was one that he approved of even though they both knew Alonzo didn't care where they sat. But that was Alonzo, and Ada, actually. They weren't the kind of parents who subscribed to the idea of tough love. They treated their children as if they were precious to them because they were. So precious that they discussed important matters with their children, they valued their input, and they let them try their hands at decision-making — small and insignificant at first, like where they sat in a restaurant, and then weightier as they grew. They didn't judge, and course correction from them was firm but loving.

Their love was solid as a rock.

Amir and Alonzo followed Kayla across the main dining area to a bank of booths. She was nice enough to keep just ahead of them to lead the way but not so fast that Alonzo felt pressured to rush. As they walked, people called out to Alonzo, which Amir was very used to, but made their route just that much slower.

"Hey, Reidy," someone called from across the room. "Where you been?"

"Living my life," Alonzo called back as he walked in his signature smooth strut. It might have been slower than it used to be, but it was there.

When they were teenagers, Amaya used to hate the way *everyone* seemed to know their parents. They couldn't go two feet in the mall without someone from the Black repertory theater stopping Alonzo to talk about the spring musical, and they never made it out of the grocery store without one of the cashiers inevitably reminding Ada that they were one of her former students. Their parents were somehow intensely regular while also being community celebrities. It was terrible, but things were different now.

These days, Amir and his sister reveled in seeing people they'd never met before or barely remembered from years ago spot their father from across the street and dart through traffic just to say hi. And if the person couldn't make the trip, they'd follow in Alonzo's wake as he went to them for a quick — but not quick at all — chat.

Amaya relished these moments especially.

She didn't talk about it — not to Amir, at least — but he knew that his sister's feelings about their parents' local celebrity had changed since they'd lost their mother. She used to sulk just out of their mother's eyesight, annoyed and desperate to be free from the bonds of casual conversation, but now she lived for those double-takes of recognition from a stranger in the supermarket. Amir could just imagine her blinking smile as she waited for them to place her face and then amble over to ask, in embarrassed but friendly whispers, "You wouldn't happen to be related to Ada Reid, would you? I swear you look just like her."

He'd seen those interactions. The way his sister's smile was bright but sad. How she had to blink back tears at their mother's name. The relief she felt when she got to say, "Yes, I'm Ada's daughter." Amir understood, or at least he tried to. His sister counted on those people to remind her that her mother had been real, to see her mother's face in her own, and to give Ada back to them for an all too fleeting moment. She craved that visceral reminder of what it had been like to be Ada Mae's only daughter.

Amir wondered if he would be the same when Alonzo was gone.

Kayla placed laminated menus onto the table and smiled at them before walking back to the front of the restaurant.

"You alright?" Amir asked Alonzo, standing as his father lowered his body into his seat. Alonzo leaned heavily on the table and the back of the booth to stabilize himself. Amir's heart was firmly lodged in his throat.

"I'm alright. Just fine," he replied in a slightly labored huff.

Amir sat only after Alonzo was settled.

They didn't actually need to look at the menu. Everyone in the Reid household knew Mama Rae's menu back to front, and Alonzo was one of the older customers who remembered a few things that used to be on the menu back in the day but had got taken off for some reason or other over the years. And because of the length of his memory, they also knew Big Thomas, the chef, would make it for the old heads and the old heads only. Still, they spent a few minutes looking over the menu, nonetheless, giving the offerings the consideration they deserved. Alonzo even pulled his glasses from his left chest pocket to peer at the laminated menu in his hands.

Amir mostly pretended to consider the laminated

paper in front of him. Like Alonzo, he knew what he was going to order before he'd even hit the freeway, but he used this moment to drown out the familiar din of the restaurant so he could focus on the sound of Alonzo's breathing. It was a habit he'd developed only after his mother's death. Sometimes, he couldn't focus on anything until he'd mentally confirmed the evenness of Alonzo's inhalations and smooth exhalations. He didn't know how not to worry.

He felt too young for this role reversal. He hadn't been ready to hover over his father in some of the ways his father had once hovered over him. And some nights, he laid awake in bed, wondering at the toll all these years of anxiety would take on him. But at the end of the day, he was grateful for the opportunity to worry.

He'd never gotten the chance to do that with his mother.

"Gonna get the shrimp and grits," Alonzo said out of the blue.

"You always get the shrimp and grits," Amir replied.

Alonzo sat back and pulled his reading glasses from his face. He looked at Amir with a small smile on his lips. He folded his glasses and placed them back inside his shirt pocket. "You sound real smug for a man who's about to get the smothered chicken with an extra piece of cornbread."

Amir's smile froze, and his father chuckled warmly in triumph. "Mmmhmm, like I thought. Glass houses, 'Mir. Glass houses.

Amir sighed and changed the subject. "Alright, so you showed up to the fair late, which is literally the worst thing you could do 'cause mama hates...hated," he corrected, swallowing hard and angling his eyes to the right over Alonzo's shoulder. "Mama hated when people were tardy. So, she read you like a newspaper."

Alonzo sighed. He used to tell his children that music was all about the nuance. The layering of sound, the unexpected crescendo, the breakdown, the guitar solo, and above all else, the way it could pull you through so many emotions in a key change. Amir heard nuance in that sigh, but he wished he didn't. He wished he couldn't decipher that grief and love and longing in such an ephemeral gust of air. But he was Alonzo's son; how could he miss it?

But then Alonzo chuckled, and all that grief and love and longing shifted to a new tempo. Emotion in a new key hit different, and he let his gaze wander back to his father's face. His smooth dark brown skin seemed even richer and darker contrasted with his gray hair, and his smile was pure nostalgia. His smile was only for Ada.

"She used to say that I couldn't be mad when she told me 'bout myself 'cause she'd been doing it longer than we'd been together. I spent thirty-eight years with that woman, and that sharp tongue never let up." His shoulders shook with more laughter. "Thank the Lord."

"So it was love at first sight?"

Alonzo shook his head and dragged himself out of the past to look at his son. "For me? Absolutely. For your mother? Absolutely not. I wasn't her type. Before me, your mama liked 'em real nerdy."

"What?"

"Oh, yeah. The cat she dated right before she met me was some accountant for the City. She used to love a man who could talk math to her."

"You're joking."

Alonzo laughed. "That's exactly what I said, but your mama loved science and math. Our first date, I took her to the Exploratorium, and I swear if there hadn't been all them kids around—"

"Pop. No," Amir cut in, his hands already moving toward his ears. "No."

Alonzo's laughter was louder, stronger, his shoulders jumping in amusement. "Anyway, she wasn't interested in me. I wasn't nerdy or smart. I was just a mess."

"Sounds like it," Amir muttered.

"Respect your elders," Alonzo said in a warning that didn't have a hint of bite.

Amir laughed. "But clearly, you changed her mind, or else I wouldn't be here. Come on, pops. Give me the rundown. How'd you do that?"

Alonzo's eyes shifted over Amir's left shoulder, and his smile sharpened slightly. Amir felt his father begin to drift slowly away.

"I was myself. Just my messy self. And I guess your mama saw something in me she liked. A little bit of potential."

1967

THE MUSIC COLUMNS in the *Voice* were legendary but not particularly varied. Stu Collins was the lead music reporter, and he covered all the rock shows, a smattering of blue-eyed soul when he was in the mood, and every now and then, a jazz show, just to keep readers on their toes. At least, that's what Alonzo thought. But other than that, anything Stu didn't want to cover, the paper doled out to a network of freelancers all over the country. Freelancers like Alonzo.

Stu had planned to cover the Monterey Pop Festival. He'd flown from New York a few weeks before to cover a few shows in Los Angeles. The plan had been to drive up north to Monterey and then head back east, following some acts he thought were just on the verge of breaking through. But then his appendix had burst the day before the festival started, and Alonzo had gotten the call up to the big leagues.

Alonzo hated to rejoice in another man's pain, but he just knew that if he could prove to Ed and Stu that he had what it took to be on staff — if he wrote something Stu liked — then life as he knew it would change. When he was little, he used to carry a handheld radio with him everywhere he went. Some kids had blankets; Alonzo had 1450 AM KDIA to keep him company, especially at night. He'd been talking and writing about music for most of his life, and he was damn good at it. All he had to do this weekend was prove it.

The festival didn't kick off until just about sunset. Alonzo had studied the bill, and he wasn't digging the lineup the first day. If he hadn't had to meet Ada, he might have driven south slowly, soaking up the vibe before strolling into the fairgrounds just before the first act took the stage. That ride would have given him the time to figure out his angle, to think about how he wanted to approach this piece, what he thought would impress Stu. But he'd been in too much of a hurry, and he couldn't help but wonder what Stu's angle had been — who he'd been interested in seeing — and it made him second-guess himself with every step. He needed to get out of his own head, but he couldn't. His entire future was riding on this weekend, and he couldn't shake the fear that he was going to fuck it up.

Maybe he'd already fucked it up.

And then there was Ada, nudging her way into his consciousness. That she didn't even want the mental real estate he was staking out for her didn't matter. It was hers. And as they walked the perimeter of the grassy field in front of the stage, it was so much easier to think of her instead of grasping for purchase at Stu's assignment.

"What's your vision?" Ada asked out of the blue. She was crouching next to him, her backpack on the ground.

He kneeled down next to her. "What do you mean?" he asked. His eyes were on her hands, so he saw when they froze. He lifted his eyes to her face. She was squinting at him in the bright sun.

"This is your first feature," she said rather than asked.

"Am I that obvious?"

"Yes."

Alonzo sighed, but Ada just smiled, shrugged, and lifted her camera from the bag. "Ed wants an insert on the Festival, an entire visual essay to go along with your piece. Stu had a vision for it."

"What— what was it?"

She threw the camera strap over her neck and shrugged again. "Doesn't matter." She zipped up her bag.

"I mean, if I knew what Stu wanted to do, then I could—"

"Then you could what? Write the story Stu wanted to write? I doubt that."

Alonzo deflated internally.

"Aw, don't pout," Ada teased, her smile unfortunately brighter than the sun in that moment.

Alonzo looked away — out of embarrassment that he was, in fact, pouting and unable to hide it, but also that he'd never wanted to kiss someone more than in that moment when she was laughing at his inadequacy. He jumped when her hand settled on his right shoulder. Her touch was light but substantial all at the same time. He turned back to her, and her smile was gone, but her face was still bright.

"Let me hip you to a piece of advice. Take it or leave it. You're not Stu. There's only one Stu, and the *Voice* only needs one Stu, so there's no reason to try and be him. You got this chance, and you can make of it whatever you want. Don't waste it trying to imitate somebody else. Write the story you want to write."

Alonzo didn't try to hide his reaction to her words. Instead, he focused on them and holding her gaze, and he tried not to look at her glossy lips. "I don't know," he finally admitted. "When Ed called, I just said yes. And then this morning, I had to get down here, so I didn't really take the time to think about what I wanted. What I was going to do."

There were moments of silence between them, even as the crowd moved around them in a loud ruckus. After a long while, Ada squeezed his shoulder and stood. Alonzo scrambled to stand with her. "Alright," she said, "then we'll think of today like a test run. I'll shoot what I think looks interesting, and tomorrow, you'll have a vision."

Alonzo's eyes widened. "Is that how it works?"

Ada shrugged into her backpack and then shrugged again as if to make clear that the shrug was for him. But he'd already guessed that. Somehow, he knew that her response would be so casual because she seemed above it all — as if nothing so banal as fear and doubt could touch her.

She lifted her camera in her hands, her long, delicate fingers wrapping around it. "Yeah," she said, "that's exactly how it works." And then she winked at him, smiled, and raised the camera to her face, pointed straight at him.

The sound of the shutter closing settled the matter and imprinted this moment in Alonzo's memory forever. He didn't know how Ada could be so confident in his ability to figure this assignment out, but he liked the idea that someone believed in him.

1967

"THAT WASN'T what I was expecting," Ada said.

The first day of the festival was over, and they were walking out of the fairgrounds into the pitch-black night. There were flickering orange glares of a few campfires on the grass for the concertgoers spending the night under the stars inside the fair. The scent of smoke was a gentle peppering in the air.

"What'd you expect?" he asked. He saw her shrug out of the corner of his eyes.

"I wanted to float away," she said.

Alonzo turned to look at her profile. Ada's dark brown skin was shining in the moonlight, looking richer in the dark — or maybe it was just that he found new depths there every time he looked. He felt lightheaded. "Yeah," he said. "I get that."

They arrived at her car far too fast for Alonzo's liking.

"So, I'll see you here tomorrow morning bright and early," she said, with only a slight hint of a warning. She unlocked her car and turned toward him. "*Inside* the gate," she added.

He smiled sheepishly and ducked his head. "Yes, ma'am."

She smiled again. She liked when he called her ma'am, but he tried not to notice that. Or at least not to notice that so obviously.

"Where you staying?" she asked.

Alonzo was normally a details man. When he did a job, he liked to do it well, but somehow, in last night's excitement and this morning's rush to get Toonie's car and get down here, he'd forgotten something crucial. "Oh," he breathed, blinking at Ada as if there were answers in her eyes.

There were not.

He cringed. "I think I'm just gonna stay in my car."

It was full night, but Alonzo could see her eyebrows shoot into her hairline. "Your car?"

He sighed, hating having to admit this and not just because he couldn't believe he'd overlooked such an important fact. "I only got the call to cover for Stu last night. I didn't have time to book a room and, to be honest, I probably couldn't have afforded a room on my own anyway. I'm only freelance, and I do a bit of handiwork on the side to make ends meet." He looked everywhere else but at her as he spoke. And then he shrugged. Unfortunately, his shoulders were tight, not nearly as casual as all of Ada's shrugs today. "It's alright," he said, desperate to end what felt like an interrogation. "It's not raining or cold, and there's a truck stop just down the way where I can probably get a shower."

"Probably?"

Yeah, as soon as the words left his mouth, he realized just how flimsy this plan sounded. "I'll figure it out," he said confidently, even as his confidence was sinking rapidly. "I always do." At least those three words were true. Alonzo had not had an easy life. Making do was all he knew.

She squinted at him for a silent second. He tried not to squirm and failed. When she finally spoke, he wished for the silent interrogation again.

"You know the *Voice* ain't ever gone give you Stu's job, right?" she said, slowly, as if she wanted to make sure that he got this message.

Alonzo flinched. He got it. He didn't like it, but he got it.

Ada kept going. "Stu's got a lock on that music section. They only hire freelancers for shows he doesn't want to cover and when he can't."

"Yeah, I know," Alonzo said.

"Then why you doing all this?" She crossed her arms in front of her chest and cocked her right hip out as if she was annoyed. "Why you driving down here at the drop of a hat and sleeping in your car? Even without a hotel room, you're probably spending more money than they'll pay you for this piece, 'cause I bet you didn't ask Ed if he was gonna give you the same rate as Stu. And you know it'll take them damn near three months to reimburse you for your incidentals."

Alonzo's gut was twisting into a knot as she spoke because he knew every word she was saying was true, but still... "I don't want to write for the *Voice* for my whole damn career," he said, which was maybe a little bit of a lie. "It's just a stepping stone."

"To where?" Ada challenged. And fuck if he didn't like the way her voice screeched into incredulity, as if she was offended on his behalf. Or maybe her own.

He crossed his arms and challenged her right back. "If the *Voice* is so damn terrible, why are you down here taking pictures for them? I bet they won't even use most of them."

"Yeah, I know," she said with a jaunty flip of her head. "And whatever they don't use is mine."

"What do you do with them?"

"Whatever I want. I sell them to other papers or print them out for posters. I got a friend who puts 'em on t-shirts. She sells them at the flea markets round the Bay, and we split the profit."

"Okay," Alonzo breathed, "so you got a whole enterprise happening?"

"I sure do. And what I'm wondering is why you don't."

Alonzo frowned at her, not because of what she said but because he was thinking. Considering. And then deciding. "Hold on," he said. "I'll be right back," he called over his shoulder as he sprinted a few rows away to Toonie's car.

The stadium lights were a little disorienting, so he got lost and had to double back out of a row of cars to orient himself. When he made it to the car, he popped the trunk. He had a bag of fresh clothes and toiletries and a couple of blankets just in case the temperature unexpectedly dipped. He fished into his duffle bag for an old issue of the *Voice*. Every time he had a column in any paper, he bought practically every issue he could find. He gave a few to friends and the hanging tendrils of his family. And he kept a few in a scrapbook, thinking one day he would frame them all. Or maybe one day, he would have too many to frame.

Sometimes, he worried this was a waste of the little money he made, but having an issue in his bag and at the ready in a moment like this made him feel as if this was worth it. The issue he pulled out of the bag was one of his first and special. He slammed the trunk closed and jogged back to Ada's car.

He hadn't been gone long; still, he worried that maybe she wouldn't be there. But when he dashed out of a row of cars, he found her just where he'd left her, leaning against her car, the driver's door open and her arms crossed over her chest.

"I'm back," he called and then immediately felt a wave of embarrassment when she turned to look at him without waving back.

He was huffing a little when he came to a stop in front of her.

She looked him up and down like she had when they met. He should have felt self-conscious, but he liked the feeling of her looking at him, teasing him, and challenging him. Alonzo didn't know what it was about Ada Carr, but he liked her, and it was simple as that. Even though she didn't seem all that impressed with him, he was *very* impressed by her.

Maybe it was the fact that she wasn't too impressed with him that tipped him right on over into infatuation.

"What's this?" she managed to ask with barely a hint of interest.

He held the newspaper out to her. Thankfully, his hand was steady. The rest of his body might have been vibrating with his heaving breaths and nerves, but at least he didn't betray himself so easily. Still, something about this moment felt important.

"My first article is on page twenty-two. I wrote it, and it was like all my life was right there in front of me on that page," he admitted pathetically. "Would you read it?"

"Why?" she asked, even though she'd already reached for it and was folding it into her grasp.

"I don't have an enterprise yet, but I do have plans," he panted.

"And you want to prove that to me?"

Alonzo pressed his lips together and inhaled through his nose. He nodded slowly. "Yeah, I think I do."

"Why?"

Alonzo thought her voice sounded breathless. "I don't know, to be honest. But I do."

The admission felt dangerous, and it didn't help that Ada didn't respond. She just looked at him, the cast of a nearby spotlight just barely illuminating them enough that he could see the darkness of her eyes but not the clarity of her expression. She watched him, and he watched her back. A few short minutes ago, Alonzo had felt bone-tired and dejected at the possibility that he'd jumped on this opportunity for nothing, but right now, he felt amazing — as if anything was possible, as if this had been the best day of his life. He watched Ada in the gray cast of the night, and as those moments of silent awareness built one on top of the other, that nervous vibration settled into something warm and thick and palpable between them. He wondered if she could feel it.

"If you turn right out of the parking lot, the first motel you see on the left-hand side of the road is mine. I'm in room 202. If you show up around seven tomorrow morning, you can shower," Ada said. As she spoke, she watched him with more of that squinting scrutiny.

"Thank you," he whispered.

"Mmmhmm," she hummed and then ducked into her car.

He moved out of the way as Ada turned her engine on and then backed out of the parking spot. He waved at her and then watched as she drove toward the exit.

He wondered if she watched him in her rearview mirror.

2010

"SO YOU WAS homeless and broke when you met mom? Maybe *that's* why you weren't her type."

Alonzo rolled his eyes. "I was not homeless. I had an apartment in Richmond with your Uncle Toonie. Worst living experience of my life, by the way. That man had a different girl through there every other weekend, I swear."

"Uncle Toonie?" Amir asked, his eyes widening in shock.

Alonzo shook his head and reached for the glass of water in front of him. "Back before that man found Allah... Let's just say he was not above taking out a restraining order to break up with a woman back in the day."

"Uncle Toonie?" Amir asked again, enunciating each word as if he could clarify the situation with inflection.

That did *not* sound like the Toonie he knew. "Does Aunt Wanda know about that?"

Alonzo laughed. "How you think they met?"

"What?" Amir didn't know what else to say about this revelation. He had so many questions but no idea how to order the words in his brain or mouth. "What?" he breathed again.

"Well, look what the cat done drug in?"

Amir and Alonzo turned at the familiar voice and found Lena walking toward them. Mama Rae's was opened by Evelyn, whose daughter, Martha, ran it after her mother's death. Martha never had any children of her own, but she'd spent years feeding any homeless person who came by for a plate, especially the kids. Lena had been one of those kids. Amir didn't know the whole story because so much of it had happened long before he'd even been a thought in his parents' heads, but by the time Martha's cataracts started to occlude her vision, Lena had already gone back to school to get her GED while working full-time at Rae's doing everything from mopping the floor and waiting tables to cooking when Martha was too tired to stand. No one was surprised when Martha left the restaurant to Lena, who was her daughter in all the ways that mattered.

All Amir's life, Lena had been, like Toonie, one of those family members for which no blood relationship was discernible or necessary.

"I know you bet not have come all the way out here to give me shit," Alonzo called.

"All the way out where? I can walk a few feet to get on your nerves. That is a pleasure. Is that my favorite nephew?" Lena trilled, turning to Amir.

Amir stood from the table and let Lena engulf him in a hug. While she leaned over to kiss Alonzo on the cheek, Amir stole a chair from a nearby table so Lena could sit. And as she usually did, she turned that chair around, spread her legs, and crossed her arms over the back of the chair, looking casual and comfortable in a way that only Lena could muster. She was, even as she strutted gracefully into her sixties, the coolest person Amir had ever known.

"Now, to what do we owe this pleasure?" she asked.

"We was packing up the house and decided to take a break," Alonzo said easily. As if leaving the home he'd shared with his wife was no big deal. Hell, it was a big deal to Amir, and he was shocked by his father's casual tone.

And apparently, so was Lena. "Packing up the house?" she exclaimed.

Alonzo rolled his eyes. "Now, don't you start."

"Don't you— Boy, what the hell is going on here?" she turned to ask Amir.

Alonzo took another sip of water, smiling over the rim of his cup at his son. Amir sighed. He knew that look. This move was his and Amaya's decision, and even though Alonzo had agreed that it was time, he would not be letting his children off the hook for suggesting it, especially if he could get even an ounce of joy out of watching them defend themselves.

"Pops is getting old," Amir said.

Alonzo choked on his water. "Ingrate," he coughed.

Amir and Lena laughed. "We just wanna make sure he's alright."

Lena looked between son and father and then back again. "So, he's moving in with your sister?"

"No, with me."

"You?"

Amir was shocked. "What's that supposed to mean?"

"No offense, but how many people go live with their sons? Especially when they're bachelors?" She shook her head. "Most boys your age can barely take care of themselves, let alone another person."

"Lena," Amir gasped.

She looked at him seriously for a few moments before bursting into laughter.

Alonzo joined her.

Amir rolled his eyes.

"I'm just playing with you, string bean."

"String bean," Alonzo gasped in laughter and then began to choke.

Amir's smile fell away. He pushed Alonzo's glass of water closer to his father's hand. "Drink some water, pop. You alright?"

It was such a normal thing, especially for Alonzo, who

loved to laugh and seemed to inspire other people to try and make him laugh. And yet, as soon as his father's hacking cough ripped from his throat, Amir's heart began to pound against his chest in panic. He knew his response was oversized, but he could castigate himself later *after* Alonzo was okay.

Alonzo eventually picked up the glass of water and drank, slowly at first and then a larger gulp when he could breathe normally.

Lena's hand covered Amir's wrist. She patted his skin slowly. "So what y'all gonna do with the house?"

Alonzo once again looked at Amir over the cup in his hand as he drank. Amir's own mouth was dry, but he swallowed and turned to Lena. "We're gonna rent it out. Amaya has a friend whose lease is about to run out, and she's looking for a place with her boyfriend and little girl."

"Well, if it don't work out, and you need some help finding a tenant, and you aren't too particular about a credit check..." Lena said.

"We ain't," Alonzo interjected.

Lena patted the older man on the shoulder. "I know. Let me know either way."

"'Preciate it."

Lena stood from her chair with a smile and waved away those words. "Please, it's the least I can do. Mama used to say y'all sold more of her peach cobbler than anybody else."

Alonzo's smile was instantaneous. "That was mostly Ada."

It was subtle, but Amir heard the wistful tone in his father's voice when he said his late wife's name as if those two syllables were each a distinctive prayer.

"Well, make sure you say bye before you go, you hear?" she said.

"Yes, ma'am," Amir said.

Lena nodded at their waiter as he made his way toward their table.

"Right on time," Alonzo breathed.

1967

"YOU'RE LATE," Ada said as soon as she opened the door to her motel room.

"You said around seven," Alonzo said. "It's seven-fifteen."

"Around seven means seven on the dot." She walked back into the room and sat on the bed. She was wearing a teal short set thing that didn't show off more skin than yesterday but did hug her hips and breasts in a way that her dress had not.

Not that Alonzo was looking.

"Does it?" he asked, stepping tentatively inside Ada's motel room and closing the door softly behind him. He was gripping his bag of clean clothes and toiletries tight in one hand, even tighter when he was not looking at Ada's backside. He kept turning toward her and glancing away quickly. She was too beautiful to stare at head-on, especially after a night of dreaming freely about her.

"Yes, it does," she said, drawing his gaze to her again. "Bathroom's that way." She tilted her head back, and her big gold hoops brushed her bare shoulders.

Alonzo turned away again. "I won't be long."

"Take your time."

He stopped and frowned at her. "But you said I was late."

She turned away from him and picked up a small mirror on the bedside table and a tube of mascara. From this angle, he could see a hummingbird tattoo on her left shoulder, a delicate outline and soft shading that made his fingers itch. He stared at it because it seemed like a safe space to rest his eyes, but it wasn't. There was so much of her beautiful skin on display, and he wanted to touch it all.

"I like a clean man," she whispered, carefully raking the mascara wand through her eyelashes.

Alonzo's eyes lifted to the mirror in her hands, and he could swear their eyes met. He opened his mouth to say... something, but no words came out.

"Hurry up," she said.

He exhaled loudly. "I wish you'd make up your mind."

Her laughter made his chest constrict. "Boy, you wouldn't know what to do with me if I made up my mind about you."

Alonzo turned and walked toward the bathroom.

"We'll see," he muttered just as he closed the door behind him.

Her laughter fell away.

▭

THE SUN WASN'T high in the sky yet. The morning air still had the tiniest bite to it, not cold but crisp. It felt fresh and sharpened everyone's anticipation as they streamed back onto the fairgrounds. Even though Ada had been annoyed that he was late, they'd arrived at the festival right on time for her to start taking pictures as the grounds filled with people.

Last night, Alonzo had gotten back to Toonie's car with a plan to follow Ada's advice and come up with a vision for his story. But as soon as he'd crawled back into the car, he'd fallen into a fitful sleep littered with dreams of Ada's face.

He didn't enjoy being back at the concert without a vision, but he couldn't deny that yesterday, Ada had freed him. He might not have a clear plan for his story, but he wasn't worried about mimicking Stu any longer, so he directed her and her camera in a way that fit his style, half-formed as it was.

"This is my favorite part of a show," he said.

She snapped a couple of quick pictures before she turned to him. "What part? Morning shows?"

"No, I mean just before the band takes the stage,

when everyone's waiting around, unsure of what to do with themselves and all the energy they brought with them."

"Why?" Alonzo liked the way Ada asked questions, straight to the point, no chaser, no explanation, with full assurance that she had the right to do so.

"It's all about the energy," he said, his eyes scanning across the lawn to make sure he didn't linger on her. "I like taking it all in. I like thinking about all the different kinds of people one show can pull into the same room. Black folk from the flats, fancy Negroes from the hills, people with money, people counting loose change to buy a bottle of beer. The people in the front row who know every word to every song. The ones you know are 'bout to sing at the top of their lungs for the whole night. The cats with a slim cigarette behind one ear who just wanna lean against the bar and catch a groove."

The camera shutter closed, and Alonzo turned to find Ada's lens trained on him again. He blinked at her as she lowered her camera.

"And which one are you?" she asked.

He swallowed and smiled shyly. "The square in the corner nursing a drink and watching everybody else get down. What about you?"

A slow smile parted her mouth. Alonzo's eyes dipped down at the flash of her pink tongue, wetting the crease of her lips. He hadn't meant to look, but once he had, he couldn't look away.

"I'm the drunk one in the front row singing every word," she said, giggling lightly.

Alonzo met her eyes and tried to laugh with her. He also tried not to look at her with heat in his eyes, but since she was looking back at him with something that he could have sworn mirrored his own expression, he decided to follow Ada's lead at least for a few seconds.

"You wanna get closer, Alonzo?" she asked in a husky whisper.

He nodded slowly.

"Well, come on," she said and then turned away.

"Wait," he whispered in confusion. "Oh. You meant closer to the stage."

She was walking backward again as if there wasn't enough time to stop and talk, but she wasn't ready to leave him just yet. Her smile had dipped into a grin. "Of course, I did. What did you think I meant?"

Alonzo felt Ada's gaze all over his skin. "No, I knew what you meant," he said, ducking his head and smiling. He wiped a sheen of sweat from his forehead and jogged to catch up with Ada once again.

"Mmmhmm, sure you did," she teased.

THEY SPENT the afternoon darting in and out of the crowd.

Technically, they didn't have to stick together. Ada

was more than capable of getting the shots she needed or thought Alonzo might need on her own, but she never mentioned them separating, and Alonzo certainly didn't want to bring it up, so they wandered around the festival hip-to-hip.

Ada Carr smelled like peaches and cocoa butter.

That wasn't what Alonzo was supposed to be thinking about, but he was. And that wasn't what he wrote in his notebook, thankfully, but it wasn't far off. They sat under a tree, enjoying a reprieve from the scorching sun and eating a lunch of fried fair food, water, and beer. While Ada changed the lens on her camera, Alonzo tried to do his job. He updated the concert lineup in his notes and jotted a few lines about the crowd's reaction to Janis Joplin's set with Big Brother and the Holding Company. He busied himself working while Ada sipped on a beer.

He'd gone back to looking at her out of the corner of his eye. And when he was done taking notes he'd have to decipher back in Oakland at his typewriter, he turned to a blank page at the back of the notebook and tried to capture Ada in words, but there weren't enough. Ada was music on two legs, and the pounding of his heart provided a beat. But he couldn't tell her that, so he wrote it down instead.

"So, what's your vision?" she asked, shocking him out of this moment.

He looked at her and then quickly away, clearing his throat before he spoke. "What's the first song you ever remember hearing?" he asked.

"What?"

He turned back to her. It was probably a bad idea, but he couldn't stop himself. "First song you remember hearing. Doesn't matter how old you were."

She furrowed her brows and frowned.

At first, he thought the look on her face was judgment, but he realized after a few seconds that it was consideration. She was taking his question seriously, and that made him feel...something.

"I don't know," she shrugged. "Must've been a lullaby. I think. Okay, yeah, absolutely. I don't know what it was, but I can remember my Nana Pat singing to me all the time when I was a baby. Sometimes she didn't even sing; she just hummed."

Alonzo was so happy he'd let himself look at her because as she spoke, Ada's eyes drifted away, and a small innocent smile brightened her face. She was so beautiful he held his breath.

When she focused back on his face, her smile faltered. "That probably doesn't count."

"It does," he rushed to say. "Now, what about high school? What's the first song that comes to mind?"

She did that adorable brow-furrowing thing again, and her smile was wobbly, but she didn't take nearly as long to answer. "Senior year. Mary Wells. 'Two Lovers.' I musta wore that forty-five out."

Alonzo's eyebrows lifted. "That's a hit."

"Sure was."

"Family?"

"His Eye Is On the Sparrow," she said without a moment's hesitation.

"Grew up in the church?"

She rolled her eyes. "Yeah. So, what's your point?"

He licked his lips and straightened his back. "I've been thinking all day that this lineup is...eclectic,' he said, trying to be diplomatic.

"Chaos," Ada corrected firmly.

"It's all over the place," he said around a soft chuckle. "If I hadn't been sent down here, ain't no way I'd've bought a ticket, you know?"

Ada nodded.

"But I'm looking around, and it's different crowds jamming to different music and then ceding the lawn for other people to jam to the music that moves them. I don't think I've ever seen anything like that."

As he spoke, Ada turned to look at the fairground green as if she was seeing it differently. Even though she'd spent hours and multiple rolls of films documenting it all, she took it all in with brand-new eyes, but he watched her.

"I think some songs just imprint on us. They sear themselves into our memories, and for the rest of our lives, whenever they come on the radio, we just go hurtling back to that moment. You'll hear that lullaby one day and remember being with your Nana Pat or sitting in church with your family or singing Mary Wells with your friends on the way to class." Her smile was pure light. "I think this concert could be one of those moments. In a year or ten years, someone's gonna hear a song by one of these bands, and they'll come hurtling back here in their minds. They'll remember this sun and the taste of cotton candy and warm beer. They'll remember the bonfire smoke in the air. Peaches and cocoa butter," he whispered before he could stop himself. "I want a piece that evokes that moment, but not in a year or ten years, right now."

She turned, and they locked eyes.

"I want to write about what it feels like to *know* that this moment is going to matter. That the rest of our lives will have spun on the needles of *this* weekend, *these* songs."

She blinked at him a few times before speaking. Her voice was hoarse. "That's your vision?" she asked. "That's what you see?"

He didn't have to lie because he was looking at her; all afternoon, Alonzo had done nothing but see Ada. "Yeah," he breathed. "That's my vision."

"Not bad," she teased. "Not bad."

1967

"YOU LIVE AROUND HERE?" Alonzo asked a Black woman in a pair of high-waisted jean shorts and a white t-shirt she'd tied under her breasts.

"Oh no, my friends and I drove in from Nevada."

"Where in Nevada?" Alonzo was scribbling down notes quickly as she spoke, the sound of Ada's camera the only thing threatening to break his concentration on this interview.

"Las Vegas. Are you from around here?" the woman asked him.

"Oakland," he said.

"Is that close?"

He looked up with a frown. "Huh?"

"It's a couple hours away," Ada said. "But his wife is very possessive." She whispered that last sentence.

"What?" Alonzo asked, whipping around to find Ada

looking seriously at his interview subject, her camera in both hands and pressed back against her rib cage.

"Wife?" the girl asked in a shriek. "He's not wearing a ring."

"Three kids, too," Ada added gravely, ignoring the other woman's valid observation.

"Ada," Alonzo hissed. When he turned back to his interview subject, he saw a confused but hungry gleam in her eye. He'd apparently missed that before, but he didn't know how because she wasn't hiding it. She was interested in him. He forced himself not to frown. "And one more on the way," he lied. "We're hoping for a girl this time."

He heard the sharp intake of Ada's breath behind him as she tried to stifle her laughter.

His interview subject pouted prettily at him. "Shame," she said before turning and flouncing away.

He and Ada watched her hips sway with each step. She turned to look over her shoulder and wave goodbye to Alonzo. He and Ada waved back.

"Can't believe you didn't notice she was flirting with you," Ada said with a pitying sigh.

"I'm working," Alonzo replied in his own weak defense. He turned, ready to plead his case to her like he so often did with Toonie. He could even taste those all too familiar excuses for why work took precedence over dating.

But Ada didn't give him a chance to defend himself. "Can't work all the time."

"Last night, you were telling me I didn't have a game plan and needed to work more. Now, you're telling me to stop and flirt with some girl I don't know who's only here for a few days to hear Jimi Hendrix. First, I was late, and then there was no rush. Can you make up your mind?"

Her laughter was all melody. "Life is complicated, Alonzo. You're just gonna have to learn to keep up," she said, turning on her heels and walking away. Alonzo thought she was switching her hips harder than the girl from Nevada, but maybe that was just his imagination.

THE DAY WAS WEARING ON, but it was still bright when Hugh Masekela hit the stage. For the first time all day, Ada let her camera dangle from her neck and danced to the music. They'd waded into the crowd. It was hotter in the throng of people — almost too hot — but he didn't want to be anywhere else in that moment. Ada was standing in front of him, smelling like peaches and cocoa butter, swaying left to right, circling her hips, her butt grazing the front of his jeans. Alonzo shoved his hands in his pockets and swayed. He was just a little offbeat from Ada, too afraid to let their bodies catch the same rhythm.

After a while, she turned to him and shook her head.

"What?" he called over the thrumming crowd and the drums from the stage.

She didn't answer his question. Not in words, at least.

She turned back to the stage and reached back for his wrists. She pulled his hands from his pockets and placed them on her waist.

Alonzo held his breath.

Ada's hips stilled for a second.

The crowd kept swaying, but they stayed still.

After a short internal battle, Alonzo exhaled and then inhaled quickly, breathing in that scent before he allowed himself to curl his fingers into her soft waist.

Her sharp exhalation was less a sigh than a moan.

His fingers dug in deeper. "This isn't professional," he said, just loud enough to hear.

"I know," she breathed, and then she began to sway. Not fast enough to catch the beat of the song yet, but after dancing around one another since the moment they met, their slow sway was like a whirlwind.

She turned her head, and he ducked down to bring his ear closer to her mouth. His mouth closer to hers. "I've done a bunch of shows with Stu," she said, confusing him at first. "He likes to hide backstage and rub shoulders with the musicians. It makes him feel important. It's boring. The show isn't backstage. It's out here with the crowd. It's in the music the band makes with their fans. The drums and the stomping of feet. It's all about the give and take."

Alonzo moved his head, and Ada moved hers. They were face-to-face now. Close enough that it wouldn't take much effort at all to taste her lips. "You read my article," he said, never having heard his own words on someone else's lips quite like this.

Her smile made his temperature rise.

"You're better than Stu," she breathed, her words ghosting over his lips.

He shook his head as a reflex but stopped when she tightened her grip on his hands.

"Don't you waste too much time at the *Voice* if they're not gonna invest in you."

"That's good advice."

"That's great advice," she insisted. "And you can thank me for it when you write your first book."

"Book?"

Ada's smile was wise yet playful. It said, 'wait and see' and 'trust me.' But even better than that smile was the feel of Ada Carr taking a step back, pressing her back to his front, and dragging his arms to wrap around her waist.

Now when she moved, Alonzo didn't have a choice but to match her rhythm, to grind into her as she ground into him, to let the music take them away together.

2010

"I THOUGHT you said you wasn't her type," Amir said.

"I wasn't. I met a couple of her exes after we started dating. Very square and very successful. I know they wasn't sleeping in their cars."

Amir took a sip of water and raised his right eyebrow at his father, a thing Alonzo usually did to him; a kind of playful, questioning judgment. "And what were you?" he asked.

"I already told you. I was a mess," Alonzo laughed. "I had plans, but I had almost as many jobs. Some days I felt like a chicken with its head cut off. But when I met your mother, I was still too terrified to want anything more than what I knew. Writing freelance was like having one foot in the door. I knew I wanted to get on staff, but I was too damn scared to let myself hope that I could before that weekend. And far as I could tell, your mama did *not* have time for brothas like me."

"*Brothas* who were still getting their sh— stuff together?" Amir put an emphasis on that first word and sounded nearly exactly like him.

Alonzo grinned at Amir's almost-curse. "Yeah, brothas like that."

"So, can I ask you a question?"

"You just did."

Amir rolled his eyes and smiled. "I'm gonna ignore your corny joke. If you weren't her type, why was she running such a smooth game on you?"

Alonzo laughed. "Running game? Busting my balls, more like."

Amir shrugged. "Everybody's game ain't the same. That's what you always told me."

He sat back and looked at his father, studying him. He didn't know what he was looking for at first, but eventually, he realized that he was trying to see him not as the older man in front of him but as the young man Alonzo had been. He didn't have to conjure that image whole cloth. Their house had been full of Ada's photographs, framed and hung around on nearly every wall to catch the best light, or lovingly placed in family photo albums on a tall shelf in the living room, or hung on a line drying in the garage Alonzo had converted into Ada's darkroom.

Ada took all kinds of photographs — events, nature,

family portraits, still life — but Ada Reid's favorite subject was her husband by a country mile. She loved her kids, but they did not love the camera, and the older they got, the less willing they were to let her turn her lens on them. Alonzo had no such qualms. He loved nothing more than making his wife happy, and if taking pictures of him made Ada happy, then he'd been more than willing to sit for her all day.

Based on all the pictures he'd seen of Alonzo throughout the years, Amir knew that his dad had been tall but not too tall, skinny but not lanky, with an afro bigger than his head. There were far too many photos of him in bellbottoms and ugly sneakers. He had big hands, a wide smile, and more often than not, a pencil tucked behind one ear.

But no matter how his fashion changed or his hair grayed, one thing remained the same. Alonzo's love for Ada was in the way he looked at her when they were standing next to one another as if the camera didn't exist, and the way he looked at the camera when she was behind it. After she died, Amir had gone through Ada's work, trying to discover some hidden depths of her through her work. What he'd found was no surprise. Ada had loved to photograph Alonzo because she had *loved* him with her entire soul. Her cameras had captured her husband — the depth of him, all his kindness and promise and beauty and softness — because she saw him that way. Their love was all over Ada's photography. The body of her work was a testament to the life she'd built with him.

So Amir was having a hard time believing that Alonzo hadn't been her type. "I bet mama had you wide open from jump," he said.

Alonzo wiped his mouth with a napkin and grinned at his son. "From the moment I met her. I might not have been her particular cup of tea, but she was mine, and I was willing to put in the work."

"All done?" their waiter asked, pointing at the table where Amir and Alonzo had already stacked their dishes.

"Yeah. Thanks," Amir said, sliding the check with a few bills on top toward him as well. "Tip's in there too."

"Thank you."

When the waiter was done, Amir turned back to his father. He looked contented, full, and a little livelier as he let his food settle. He hated to ruin the serenity of the moment, but they really didn't have that much time left in the house, and the issue of those records wouldn't solve itself.

"So y'all met at this festival, and the records are like... what?" Amir asked as gently as he could.

Alonzo shook his head easily. "Ain't done with the story yet."

"I get the gist."

"Can't get the gist of love, knucklehead." Alonzo rolled his eyes and turned to scoot out of the booth. He was grumbling lightly as he did so, but he held his breath as he pushed to his feet.

Amir held his breath as well. "Didn't mama used to say something like that?" Amir asked.

His father was breathing a little harder than Amir thought he should. He wanted to ask if he was alright, but he figured Alonzo wouldn't like that, so he gripped his thighs under the table. He watched his father's hands intently as they grasped the table and back of the booth. He held on as he caught his breath.

Alonzo took a few slow breaths before he responded. "How she say that when I just made it up?"

Amir rolled his eyes. "I said *something like*."

Alonzo turned to him and stared for a few seconds before his face lit up, and he shook his head. "You're thinkin' of that Supremes song. She used to dance around the kitchen, making pancakes on Saturday morning, playing one Supremes record after another. Remember that?"

Amir felt his chest relax as he nodded because, yeah, he did remember that. He could probably close his eyes and smell those chocolate chip pancakes and hear his mama's voice, beautiful but just a little bit off-key. And suddenly, he was blinking back tears.

Alonzo nodded. "Your mama got every record Diana Ross ever released with the Supremes and after in that living room," Alonzo said, but then his face fell. "Had," he corrected. "They're still there, but I mean—"

"I know what you mean, pops. It's okay." Amir felt as desperate for his father not to have to stumble through the rest of that sentence as he was not to hear it. Alonzo had a way with words. When Amir was a boy, he used to love sitting at his father and Toonie's feet while they talked about...everything, weaving stories about their youth and their old neighborhoods that were so vivid Amir could see them in his mind. But for the past five years, Alonzo had been tripping over his words whenever he talked about Ada, fudging the present and past tenses as his mind struggled to describe life without her only to retreat into the past where he didn't have to pull such cruel phrases together.

It was painful to watch.

"Oh, good. I caught y'all." Kayla was rushing toward them with a plastic bag in her hands, and Amir stood from the booth.

"Lena wanted me to give this to you."

"That a cobbler?" Alonzo asked with a raised eyebrow.

"Yes, sir," she beamed.

"Alright now."

"We can't—" Amir said.

"The hell we can't. Take the cobbler, boy."

Kayla giggled and stretched her arms toward Amir.

He sighed as he took the pan from her. "Let me pay for it, at least."

"It's a gift, boy," Lena called across the restaurant. She was behind the counter, cashing someone out but still managing to keep an eye on them. A few people stopped eating and turned to see who she was yelling at, but for the most part, Mama Rae's was full of regulars who just assumed that whoever Lena was calling out deserved it.

"I tried to tell him," Alonzo said.

When Amir turned, Alonzo was halfway toward the door, moving slow but steady on his way.

"Pop," Amir said, walking after him, his heart pounding. "Slow down."

Alonzo waved over his head. "Can't get no slower than me these days."

Amir rolled his eyes, even though he was right; he caught up with him in a few steps. They both waved to Lena, and Amir pushed the door open for his father.

Outside, it was a perfect Bay Area day; overcast, warm, but not hot. Mild. Alonzo stopped, put his hands on his hips, and stretched his back, closing his eyes as he lifted his head toward the sky.

"You alright?" Amir finally allowed himself to ask for the hundredth time today. He braced himself for the sound of his father sucking his teeth, annoyed, but it didn't come.

"I'm fine, Amir. Just old. We all just getting older and older every day. That's life." He sighed, and the contour of that sound was like a punch to the gut.

Alonzo was right; Amir knew that. Every day he knew he had less time with his father than the day before, and one day, it would all be gone. One day, he'd lose Alonzo like he lost Ada, and all that would be left were those pictures and Alonzo's books and wedding bands he'd probably wear on a chain around his neck. It wouldn't be enough. Those pictures wouldn't suck their teeth or remind him to watch his language. Those books couldn't place a big hand on his shoulder and squeeze, reassuring him that he'd made a good choice and that his father was proud of him. There was a lump in Amir's throat, and he looked away, closing his eyes against another all too sudden wave of tears.

When his father's hand settled on his right shoulder, Amir swallowed a sob.

"Come on, let's get back to the house," Alonzo said gently and squeezed. "We got cobbler to eat."

Amir nodded.

"I'll tell you about your mother getting me high," Alonzo offered in a light voice as his hand slipped away.

Amir turned to him with a frown. "She'd never."

Alonzo's laugh was so loud he seemed nearly a decade younger. "The hell she wouldn't. That woman was always corrupting me. Not that I minded."

"Pops. No," Amir said as he followed his father to the car.

1967

"I DON'T KNOW," Alonzo said, "we're working."

Ada dipped her fingertips into the plastic bag of bud in her lap and sprinkled it into the rolling paper cradled in her other hand, carefully, as if she was making a gourmet dish.

Alonzo liked the way concentration looked on her face, her top lip trapped between her teeth, her eyes narrowed, her chest still. Not that the seriousness of her task stopped Ada's sharp tongue.

"So you're a square," she laughed mockingly.

"I'm not a square."

"You sure about that? Look, if you don't smoke, just say so. I won't hold it against you." Her gaze lifted from the joint she was constructing, and she winked. "Promise."

Alonzo sighed and looked away. Night had fully fallen. They'd staked out a patch of grass near enough to the stage to see the act but not close enough to be crushed in the thick of the crowd. The problem wasn't that he didn't smoke; the problem was that the idea of passing a joint from his mouth to Ada's and back again had made him hard the minute she'd pulled that baggie from her backpack.

He also didn't think he could trust his body to behave. Alonzo had a loose tongue when he smoked. Or, as Toonie said, "You just don't ever shut the fuck up when you high. I ask you one question, and you be talking all night." He didn't want Ada to see him like that. He didn't really think he had a chance with her, but if he did, he didn't want to ruin it because he couldn't stop telling her everything he knew about Black musicians in bluegrass or listing every Motown artist by year.

But he couldn't tell her that he was a motormouth, so he avoided her question altogether and went back to watching her hands instead.

He thought watching her roll the joint would be safe. It was not.

Her fingers, like the rest of Ada, were delicate, long and slender. She used her fingertips to break up the small particles of marijuana, moving from the bag to the rolling paper and back again in measured movements. She carefully massaged the weed, evenly distributing it inside the paper with the same kind of focus as he'd seen earlier today as she'd directed her camera at the crowd.

And then there was her tongue, wetting the rolling

paper in one long, slow swipe before those fingers began to roll.

Every muscle in Alonzo's body tensed painfully. All the blood in his body headed south. Every thought he'd had today that wasn't about Ada was gone.

There was only Ada Carr.

"You can be straight with me, Alonzo," she said. "Come on, just say it. Tell me you're a square." Her voice was pure molasses, thick and sweet, a slow drawl that made him wonder where her people were from. But her words were sour provocation, meant to sting, but maybe only just a little before she soothed.

He lifted his eyes from the joint to her face to find her staring at him as she rolled it closed.

"You get on your man's nerves like this?" he rasped, trying to find some purchase in this exchange.

"You trying to find out if I got a man?" she bit back quickly, throwing him off-balance once again.

"Would you tell me if you did?" He was watching her hands again.

"I'm an honest woman," she said.

He saw a small smile grace her lips, but he refused to focus on that. He couldn't. "Is that an answer?"

"Would be if you'd asked a direct question."

His eyes flitted up to hers, but she wasn't watching him now; she was inspecting the joint carefully, making sure it was perfectly formed with no tears.

And then her tongue appeared again. Alonzo was too

wound up to do anything but swallow the whimper in his throat and hope she couldn't hear the soft squeak that escaped his lips.

Alonzo had seen so many beautiful things in his life, and he regularly reminded himself of them when he needed to remember that life wasn't always bad. The sequoias in high summer. The redwoods on the rainiest day. A rainbow cutting through wet, oil-slicked streets. But none of that could hold a candle to Ada Carr, her deep brown skin, those mahogany eyes, and her bright pink tongue, poking between her white teeth and smoothing soft as butter across the thin paper to seal it closed.

She literally took his breath away.

"One toke," he breathed, transfixed.

Her tongue trailed off the edge of the rolling paper as if she was savoring the taste, as if she wanted to torture him with thoughts of what *she* tasted like. And she was.

"I'm not impressed by men who try to impress me," she said.

"Now I know that's a lie."

"Told you I don't lie."

"That mighta been a lie too, all I know."

Her smile tricked him into thinking the sun hadn't set.

She held the joint out to him in one hand and her lighter in the other. It was a challenge. He took it.

Alonzo held Ada's gaze as he placed the joint between his lips. Her eyes didn't waver, but her lashes did flutter, and he felt that movement in his gut. He flicked his thumb over the ridged edge of the lighter, and the flame came to life between them.

Ada sucked in a sharp breath as Alonzo inhaled deeply.

He held the smoke in his lungs and handed the joint back to her.

She took it, and their fingers brushed together. She lingered. Alonzo exhaled slowly, the thick smoke obscuring their vision of one another, but not the sure knowledge that the other person was still there, that they were in this moment together. Her eyes stayed on him as she brought the joint to her mouth, her lips closing over the slightly damp paper where his mouth had been. The smoke wafted in the air between them, making this moment feel otherworldly.

He wanted to tell her that. He was about to tell her that, even though the weed hadn't yet hit his system. The words were already filling up his mouth, not because he was high but just because he wanted to tell Ada everything about him and every thought that filtered through his head. He wanted Ada to know him because he wanted to know her.

"I'm single," she said on the sexiest smoky exhale. "Not looking to date." She passed the joint back to him.

"Me either," he lied.

She licked her lips, and he shifted uncomfortably. She smirked, dipping her head forward, reminding him that he was letting the weed burn out.

He took a hurried breath in, the smoke singeing his lungs, as Ada lifted onto her knees.

When her hands landed on his shoulders, he huffed out a breath before he got the chance to really inhale.

"So you smoke?" she asked, throwing one leg over his waist.

He nodded up at her, leaning back on his hand even though he wanted to place that palm on her waist again.

"But you let me call you a square? 'Cause you didn't want to smoke with me?" She didn't seem hurt, just like she was filtering through new information to arrive at her own conclusion. She plucked the joint from his fingers and took a drag as she lowered herself down into his lap.

He moaned. He couldn't stop himself.

She smiled, a thin tendril of smoke escaping between the sexy O of her parted lips.

"I—" The single word was all he could muster before Ada moved her head back and released the smoke in her mouth straight into the sky. "Fuck," Alonzo breathed.

"You?" she asked. Teased, more like. "Fuck?" She laughed as she lowered her head and then ground down to settle her ass firmly, unmistakably onto his dick.

He swallowed a groan but just barely. "Okay, I believe you don't have a man."

She shook her head and brought the joint back to her lips.

Alonzo had to look away. He couldn't watch her take this drag directly, not when her pussy was so damn close to his dick. So he watched her mouth out of the corner of his eye and tried not to let his body betray his reaction to the surprising shock of Ada on top of him.

She exhaled a beautiful plume of smoke, but she didn't pass the joint back to him. "I don't get you, Alonzo Reid."

Her words shocked him, and he turned back to her. "Are you trying to get me, Ada Carr?"

A cymbal tissed, and a ripple of excitement moved through the crowd, but all that was happening elsewhere. Here there was only Alonzo and Ada in their own little bubble, making their own music.

"I shouldn't be," she said, "but I'm doing it anyway."

There were so many questions he wanted to ask in that moment. And he guessed there were probably just as many questions Ada seemed to want to ask right back. But for all her brashness and all his yearning, neither of them said a word.

Instead, Ada slipped the joint between her lips, and Alonzo didn't pretend as if he was looking elsewhere.

Her chest expanded, and the burning orange tip of the joint illuminated a small circle of the space between their faces. He inhaled with her.

She placed her left palm flat on his chest and pressed into him.

Alonzo exhaled. Ada did not.

She leaned forward slowly, deliberately. And even though he'd spent all day wanting just this, he didn't meet her. He waited for Ada to come to him, afraid that if he made a move, he'd ruin whatever this was, and he couldn't risk that. Ada Carr was touching him and looking at him, and now that cymbal tiss had turned into a soft thrum over a drum and a plucking, exploratory bass beat. If there was ever a more perfect moment in Alonzo's life, this wiped it out of his mind completely.

Her hand moved over his shoulder as she leaned forward. The tips of her breasts met his chest.

Alonzo opened his mouth to...do...or say...something.

Ada smiled as her face descended on his, and her lips parted just enough to show him the white smoke in its depths.

The dark pools of her eyes were bright with the reflection of a constellation of stars. And finally, Alonzo stuttered into action. His arms wrapped around her waist, and he pulled her forward, crushing her breasts firmly into his chest just as her mouth covered his.

They both moaned as their lips touched. She blew the smoke from her mouth into his. He gladly accepted.

Her hand crushed the back of his afro, digging deep into the soft crown of his hair. They crushed their lips together. Alonzo was not usually a fan of shotgunning, but with Ada, it was better than he'd ever imagined.

She scratched lightly at his scalp, and he could have sworn that he felt that touch circling the base of his dick.

He moaned into Ada's mouth, and her tongue dipped between his lips, but only for the briefest taste.

Alonzo found himself leaning forward, chasing Ada's quickly retreating mouth.

When their lips finally broke apart, he exhaled the residual smoke from his lips. The air cleared between them, and he found her sitting above him with another of those mocking smiles that he was rapidly coming to adore.

And then horns ripped through the night.

"Oooh shit, I love this song!" Ada yelled, jumping to her feet.

Alonzo felt Ada's absence like a quick cut to his soul. He missed the weight of her, the smell of peaches, cocoa butter, and marijuana, the brush of her warm skin against his, the taste of her tongue. He felt sluggish now that she was gone, and she'd barely touched him. He felt woozy and hungover after the tiniest taste, and he wondered what that loss would feel like tomorrow or the week after that or a year from now.

He looked up at her, jumping in the air and swaying to the beat. In that moment, he knew, as sure as he knew his own name, that if he spent too much time with Ada, losing her would hurt. She would hollow him to the core. Normally, he would take the overwhelming feeling of loss as instructive and move on. Under normal circumstances, Alonzo might have felt something maybe half as strong as he felt in this moment, and he would run away.

She turned to look down at him with a grin. She shook her shoulders and turned in a circle. "You gon' sit there all night?" she yelled.

Alonzo didn't want to run away from Ada.

⸺

"POP, I love you and mama, but I definitely did not need to know most of that," Amir said with a frustrated sigh, both hands gripping the steering wheel uncomfortably. He normally drove with one hand on the wheel and one at his waist — the same pose Alonzo used to strike behind the wheel — but hearing his father describe his mother shot-gunning some old-timey cannabis had him on edge.

Go figure.

Alonzo's window was down, even though they were on the freeway, and he was resting a bent elbow on it. "What part was too much?" Alonzo asked, his voice nothing but faux innocence. "The weed?"

"And the...other stuff too."

Alonzo sucked his teeth and waved a hand dismissively. "Boy, please. How the hell you think you and your sister got here?"

"Magic," Amir deadpanned. "Immaculate fucking conception."

"Watch your mouth and take that exit."

"You want me to take the streets back to the house?"

"No, I wanna see the water," Alonzo breathed, turning to look out the window toward the blue bay in the distance.

2010

AMIR PULLED his car into a parking spot on the edge of Jack London Square, just down the street from the Amtrak station. The overflow parking lot had the most unobstructed view of the water as he could get. Every now and then, a person strolled in front of the car, but Alonzo didn't seem to mind. If he saw anything at all, Amir imagined he saw his late wife in his mind's eye on so many of the trips they took down here, which were too many to count. They used to come here for a date night to Yoshi's to hear some jazz and have a few drinks. They brought the kids to one of the restaurants for a special seafood dinner when they made honor roll. Or hell, maybe he was remembering the night of Amir's junior prom when he and his best friend Jay somehow ended up at Jack London in the middle of the night, tipsy and confused about which night bus would get them home.

Amir remembered that night a little too often for his liking. Ada had been silently furious in her disappointment in the front passenger seat. She'd expected better of him and couldn't imagine that he hadn't expected better of himself. Her silence was a heavy thing, and it started burning through the alcohol left in his blood. Alonzo was not the silent type. He'd looked in the rearview mirror at the boys and told them to, "Get ready for some manual labor this summer," with a good-natured chuckle. And then he'd pulled into a twenty-four-hour McDonald's to buy them some food while squeezing Ada's knee with his free hand.

He'd been too drunk and tired and young to think about it at the time, but in hindsight, Amir had come to reconsider Ada's rage. The disappointment was real, but as an adult, he recognized her uncharacteristic silence for what it most likely had been. Fear. Ada hadn't had a problem expressing herself, but fear could be paralyzing. Amir knew that now, every time Alonzo stumbled over a curb or laughed so hard, he wheezed. He wished he could go back in time and tell his mother what he'd learned.

He also wished he could find a space in the city that didn't trigger these kinds of memories, but that was impossible because Ada was everywhere in this city, memories of her threatening around every corner. For as long as he was here, he knew he would never stop missing her. He'd never get past his grief.

Alonzo sure hadn't.

He turned to his father and lifted his eyebrows.

"Alright, so who was playing at the concert?"

"Festival," Alonzo corrected.

"Festival," Amir said with a shake of his head and a shrug because what was the difference? Not that he would ask his father that question for real. That would only get him the most boring semantics lecture ever. He'd sat through more than a few of those in his life, and he did not care. It was so much easier to just capitulate and move the story along.

"It was the Sixties," Alonzo said. "Summer of Love. The lineup was eclectic, you know. Simon & Garfunkel, the Steve Miller Band, The Who, The Grateful Dead."

"Doesn't really sound like you and mom's style."

Alonzo shrugged. "Lou Rawls, Otis, and Jimi were there, too, but people are complex, 'Mir. Don't you forget that. Me and your mama weren't always your parents." He frowned through the front windshield for a second and then undid his own seat belt. "Anyway, we were there for work. We didn't need to like the music to do our jobs. And let me tell you, your mama was all about her money in those days."

Amir scoffed. "In *those* days? You know it was easier to prove I could pay my mortgage to the bank than convince mama to let me borrow five dollars."

Alonzo chuckled softly. "I know that's right. You know, when I asked your mama to marry me, she said yes, on two conditions."

"Oh, yeah?" Amir had never heard this story before.

Alonzo nodded, still looking out of the window at the bay. It wasn't the prettiest bit of water, but it was home.

"I was running around for a full two weeks trying to get everything together. I wanted to make it special for her. Told your Uncle Toonie to spend the weekend with whoever the hell he was dating then. Got a fresh cut. Cleaned the house. Cooked her dinner."

Amir shifted his body toward his father and rested the side of his head on the headrest to watch him, trying to imagine these events playing out in real time.

"And she showed up, pretty as you please, of course. Afro all big, just a little bit of makeup, not that she ever needed it. And I said, 'Ada Carr, will you spend the rest of your life with me?' as soon as she walked in the door. Didn't even let her put her purse down. Didn't even let her see the food I'd been cooking for her all day. I was so nervous and excited, I couldn't wait.

And she looked at me for a few moments that felt like an hour. She was doing that thing where she squinted at you and looked you up and down, you know?"

"Oh, I know," Amir said. "It was like you were transparent, and she could see every thought you were having or had ever had."

Alonzo laughed as he continued. "She could make your knees turn to jelly with a look. And finally, she said, 'Alonzo Reid, I'll accept your proposal, but I don't ever wanna be poor. I been poor. I'm only a block away from poor now, but I ain't having kids in poverty. I want my kids to have more than me. And if you ain't ready to do what it takes to make that happen, then maybe we aren't heading down the same path."

Amir's heart clenched.

Alonzo smiled and turned to look at his son. "Of course, I agreed. What else was I gon' say? 'No, actually, I want my kids to struggle like we did?' Money wasn't the point. She just never wanted you to struggle. Maybe we coulda been clearer 'bout that last part." Alonzo shook his head and reached out to gently pat his son's face. "But her second condition was the important one. That was the one that mattered most to both of us."

Amir moved his hand over his father's and held it to his face, imprinting the feel of his rough, calloused palm on his skin. He couldn't remember the last time Alonzo had touched his face like this, and he didn't want to forget. He couldn't forget.

Alonzo's eyes were wet, shimmering with tears and emotion that Amir couldn't fathom. His own vision began to blur.

"Your mama said every day with me had been like a love song on repeat, and she made me promise that we'd build a life like that for our kids. And we did that. Didn't we?"

Amir nodded, tears falling down his face. "You did, pops," he said, his voice breaking on a choked sob. "You did."

Amir had still been a skinny kid with ashy, knobby knees when he realized just how singular Alonzo was. When he looked at his friend's fathers, so many of them were loving in the kind of terrified way that needed to prepare their children for the harshness of the world. But Alonzo was nothing but warmth. He was the kind of parent who sat his kids down and talked them through their punishment in excruciating detail. He cried every time he listened to Sam Cooke with a glass of Hennessy. And the only time Amir could remember Alonzo yelling was in the bleachers at an A's game. Alonzo and Ada knew how hard the world could be on two Black kids, and so they gave them nothing but softness and love. It made Amir's heart clench to know that love and security had been their only plan.

Amir's phone rang, and he pulled himself together enough to lift his hips and pull his cell from his back pocket.

Alonzo's hand fell away from his son's face. He reached into his pants pocket and pulled out a handkerchief to wipe his face.

"Ah, shit," Amir breathed when he saw the name on the screen.

"Language," Alonzo muttered.

Amir used his shirt to dry his own face as he answered the call on speaker.

"Where the hell are you? And where the hell is dad?"

"Language," Alonzo said, loud enough to be heard.

"Sh— Sorry, daddy. I was just worried," Amaya replied.

"Mmhmm," Alonzo muttered, but there was already a smile on his face. "We went to Mama Rae's for lunch, we're on our way back now."

"And y'all didn't call me?" Six years ago, Amaya would have said something like that with a big smile on her face and a spoiled gleam in her eye, all that hurt nothing but a gentle tease. But ever since their mother had died, Amir had noticed the way her smile dimmed and her gaze sharpened in these moments where she felt left out. She hadn't said it in so many words, but Amir knew his sister's heart as well as he knew his own.

When Ada was alive, Amaya had felt as if she had a place. She was Ada's legacy like Amir was Alonzo's, but Ada was gone, so where did she fit now?

Certainly, it was much more complicated than that. They'd both gotten their parents' love of art but translated it in their own new ways. Amaya painted and every now and then dabbled in writing poetry and prose to channel her creative energies, which made Alonzo very happy. Amir had gone into graphic design, a thing Ada had been surprisingly proud of and awed by.

"*My baby is making real money with his art,*" she'd said because that was a very Ada thing to say.

But Amir and Amaya had inherited so many other things from their parents. Amaya had Alonzo's fat knees and big laugh. Unlike Amir, who seemed to grow into his father's twin more and more each day physically, someone who knew could look at Amaya and just as surely pick out Alonzo's blueprint as Ada's. Once upon a time, Amaya had loved that; she had reveled in being the best of both of her parents. But now that Ada was gone, Amaya seemed to be looking for their mother in herself more and more each day. For five years, she'd been trying to figure out how she fit in their shrunken family as if Ada had been her anchor in a way no one — not even Amaya — had realized until she was gone.

"Lena gave us a cobbler," Alonzo said.

Amaya's voice brightened. "I love cobbler."

Alonzo laughed. "I know you do, baby girl. And I'm pretty sure I got some ice cream in the freezer."

"I'll check," she said, hurrying off the phone.

Amir turned the key in his ignition. Before he put the car in drive, he turned to his father. "Pop, are you good with this move? I know it's late, but still."

Alonzo was watching the water again. "First time I ever danced with your mama — properly — was to Otis Redding. We was high as hell, and it was the first best night of my life. I had so many damn good nights with your mother long before that house." He reached over to pat Amir's forearm without looking. "I'm just fine. I promise."

"Language," Amir teased as he pulled out of the parking spot.

Alonzo's laughter sounded a lot like a sigh.

1967

Some concerts are difficult to describe to those who
weren't there.
The impossibility of being able to fully convey the energy
of a performance, the mood of the crowd, and the way
those two things clashed together to make magic, is the job
of a critic, but sometimes we fail.
Sometimes, the music is so good, so big, and the magic is so
out of this world that human language isn't vast enough to
capture it all.
And yet, they both live on.

Long after the band has packed up their instruments and
left town and the crowd has scattered around the world,
all that music and magic is still in the air. It sinks into the

venue floor, drips into the foundation, and hits the dirt.
The magic from that night grows roots and lives on,
forever watered by the next gig and the next gig and
so on.

The best magic, like the best music, burrows under the
skin and digs down deep. By the time the last chords
reverberate through the air, everyone in attendance is
carrying that magic with them.
That's what the Monterey Pop Festival was like. It wasn't
so much each individual performance as the sum total of
each band and every person in attendance.
The magic they made is in our marrow now.
I can't wait to see what fruit that music will bear.

"The Monterey Pop Festival Was a Magical Weekend and
Deserves to Be Remembered"
by Alonzo Reid
Staff Reporter
Village Voice, August 1967

"OOH, THIS IS MY SONG," Ada yelled again as if Otis
could hear them from the lawn. She lifted her hands into
the air and began swaying back and forth, a slow and
steady seduction that made Alonzo's knees weak now that
he was standing and the joint was hitting. He felt like he

was floating. As long as he didn't drift away from Ada, though, he had no complaints.

Alonzo's body was a riot of desire. His pulse was pounding on beat with her hips. And his tongue was sticking to the roof of his mouth, desperate to recover that briefest taste of her. His fingers were itching to pull his notebook from his back pocket so he could scribble out a few more lines about her without pretense. He needed to discover the language that could adequately capture the beauty of the blue-black tinge of her skin now that the sun had set so he could explain the way she radiated from within. He didn't need the sun in Ada's presence, but he would find a less trite way to describe that in revisions. But he couldn't stop to write because he didn't want to take his eyes off of her.

She swayed in a circle, and her face lifted in delight when they made eye contact. "That weed taking you down?" she asked.

It took a few seconds for him to process her words, and he shook his head at the speed of a snail.

Her laughter wrapped around him like a blanket as she swayed back to face the stage.

Alonzo reached for her. He was never normally so bold, but he'd wanted to touch Ada all day, even when he *was* touching her, and especially now that he'd already felt her weight on top of him.

She smiled over her shoulder as his fingers dug into her waist.

There was probably a barb on the tip of her tongue, and a not-so-small masochistic part of him wanted to hear it. He wanted to open his chest and let her cut him to kindling if it made her laugh again. But whatever she'd been about to say, he never heard it.

Horns cut into the night. This was Alonzo's song, but he didn't need to tell Ada that. Not with words, at least. Ada let him pull her to him. He turned her until they were chest-to-chest. He wrapped an arm around her as she snuggled her face into the crook of his neck, her breath making goosebumps erupt all over his skin. He held her left hand close to his chest as the song unfolded.

If I could only make you understand.

Peaches and cocoa butter.

A deep rasp that made the hair on their arms stand up.

Fire and marijuana in the air.

Her heart beating an offbeat staccato against his chest.

His own pulse an even, crooning note.

The feel of her breath against his skin.

Her name on his lips, a careful whisper into her ear.

The slow vibration of a shudder running through her body.

Your one and only man.

2010

"MAYA," Alonzo called as soon as he pushed the front door open. He ushered Amir inside first.

"I'm in the kitchen," she called back.

"You gon' tell her not to yell?" Amir asked in petty little brother annoyance.

Alonzo laughed and shook his head. His gait was a little stiff, but nothing Amir was too worried about after the longer-than-expected drive. Amir shouldered the front door closed, the peach cobbler secure in his hands, and followed Alonzo into the open-plan kitchen and little dining room at the back of the house.

"Was there ice cream in the freezer?" Alonzo asked instead of reprimanding his daughter.

Amir sighed audibly.

"Yep. And there's just enough for the three of us if we

don't give 'Mir too much," she said, gesturing toward the round dining room table.

Amir rolled his eyes and sighed, not that anyone acknowledged him.

Amaya had placed bowls and silverware out for them. This wasn't the first time they'd eaten at the table without Ada, but Amir was always surprised when he didn't see his mother there. He could still picture her reclining in her regular seat next to Alonzo's, close — close enough that she could pick off his plate when she wanted, and he could easily lean back in his chair and wrap an arm around her shoulders. Close enough that the two of them had never had to miss the other.

Amir had to look away from that empty chair. He placed the cobbler on the table and began to unwrap it.

Amaya pulled Alonzo into a hug. "You want to put the cobbler in the oven for a little bit?" Alonzo asked Amaya.

Amir waited for their instructions, feeling all of twelve and gangly again.

"Nah," Amaya said. "I like it when it's room temp. Is that bad?"

Amir opened his mouth to answer her question, but Alonzo caught his eye and raised a brow in warning. Amir clapped his lips shut and rolled his eyes. Even though he knew Amaya was still just a little bit fragile, the little brother in him couldn't help but want to annoy her, and he was a little mad Alonzo was robbing him of the opportunity.

"Nothing wrong with room temperature cobbler," Alonzo said carefully. "Have a seat. Both of you. I'll serve. Amir, you scoop the ice cream."

"Oh," Amaya said, dropping into the chair that had always been unofficially hers, on the other side of the chair that was still Ada's. "I like the sound of that."

Amir rolled his eyes yet again.

"Don't roll your eyes, boy," Alonzo joked, reaching for the cobbler.

"Yeah, Amiri," she teased, using his childhood nick-name, "don't roll your eyes."

"And don't you tease him, Amaya. Ain't y'all grown yet?"

Amir and Amaya glared at one another over the carton of ice cream.

Alonzo chuckled again. "Maybe next year."

"How's the packing coming, daddy?" Amaya asked.

Alonzo pried the paper lid off the foil container. The syrupy sweet-spicy scent of peach cobbler made Amir's mouth water.

"Can I get a piece with more crust, pops?" he asked as usual.

"Gimme his extra peaches, please," Amaya said at nearly the same time.

"I know. I know," Alonzo said, scooping out the dessert for his children as they liked before passing the bowls to Amir for ice cream.

"Packing's going alright," he finally said. "We're on track to be done tomorrow. Ain't that right, Amir?"

"Yeah. We should. Just as soon as we figure out what to do with those records." Amir nodded behind Amaya into the living room.

The room was nearly empty now, but in the past, it had been filled to the gills. Amir could hear the record player hum and feel the stomping of dancing feet in his bones. He could smell his mom's roast chicken and yams. He could smell the faint hint of smoke from people ducking outside for a quick puff on a cigarette. This room was a mosaic of memories. It would never really be empty in his mind.

But those records were all that remained of all the life they'd lived in that room and this house.

"You have to put them in storage, right? Some of them, at least?" Amaya asked, glancing at the records and then back to the bowl of cobbler in front of her.

Amir dug his spoon through the scoop of ice cream down into the flaky crust with more determination than was necessary. Once he'd shoved a bit into his mouth, he and Amaya turned to their father.

Alonzo shook his head at his children. "Where'd I leave off in the story?" he asked with a sigh and a playful smile on his face.

"You finally put a move on mom," Amir added helpfully.

"Ew," Amaya said. "Why are you telling stories about hitting on mom?"

Alonzo's sigh was really a soft chuckle. "A good story is a good damn story," he said with a shrug.

1967

"I THINK I got some good pictures today," Ada said, staring up at the night's sky as they walked back to their cars. "Damn, the stars are beautiful."

"Oh, yeah?" Alonzo mumbled, without a single ounce of care for those pictures or how the sky looked tonight because he was far too preoccupied with her.

"I won't know 'til I develop them, but I can feel it when I get a good one. No, a great one." Her voice was soft and wistful, and it drifted up into the air like those tendrils of smoke. It was dark enough that even with him being so close, some of her features were in shadow. Still, Ada's silhouette took Alonzo's breath away.

"Can you?" His voice was hoarse with need, and his heart was thumping against his chest. "Can you really feel it?"

Ada turned to him. He could feel her questioning gaze

more than he could see her eyes, just like he could hear the smile in her voice more than he could see it on her face. "You sleeping in your car again?" she asked.

Alonzo looked away, embarrassed. "Uh, yeah. I should have asked at the motel this morning if they had any rooms. I didn't think."

"Wouldn't have mattered. They don't. You could stay on the fairgrounds. Lots of people are."

"Uh, no thanks. That's not really my type of scene."

Ada's shoulder brushed his, and he turned to her again. "You wanna stay with me?"

His eyes widened, and his mouth dropped open. "What? I mean...what?"

Her laughter was featherlight. "I do have two beds," she reminded him. "It's not a huge sacrifice."

"Are you sure?" They'd arrived at Ada's car and turned to face one another. Ada leaned against her car casually, but Alonzo's stomach was tied in knots.

"Wouldn't have offered if I wasn't," she said.

That didn't help ease the tension in his body, and her answer made him remember her admonition this morning about asking a direct question to get a direct answer. "Okay. Well, yes, I'd like that. Thank you."

She shrugged. "No problem. Meet you there?"

Alonzo nodded eagerly and started to turn away.

"Alonzo."

He lifted his head and met her eyes again. "Ada?"

She licked her lips and ran a hand just over the top of

her afro as if steeling herself. "You can have the spare bed if you want, or..."

Alonzo's eyes were wide again, and those knots in his stomach were now knotting on top of themselves. "Or?"

She clearly heard the way his voice shook, and it made her smile. Of course. "Or you can—"

<hr>

2010

"NO," Amir said, standing abruptly from his chair and reaching for Alonzo's empty bowl.

"Absolutely not," Amaya echoed, handing her bowl to her brother. She pushed up from her seat while shaking her head vigorously. "Not at all." She grabbed the cobbler container and followed Amir to the kitchen.

Alonzo sat back in his chair, laughing hard enough to bring tears to his eyes. While his children cleared the table and washed up, he sat, smiling, staring at the empty chair next to him, thinking of Ada, but not as she'd been in that chair for all the years when this house had been theirs. No, Alonzo crossed his arms over his chest and rested his chin against his left shoulder and thought of Ada as she'd been that night: young, bold but still a little bit nervous, and even more beautiful than every star in the sky.

1967

"OR YOU CAN STOP WAITING for me to make all the moves," Ada said. Her eyes were dark pools in an already dark night. Her gaze bored into him, challenging and beseeching at the same time.

She was nothing but contradictions, and Alonzo couldn't get enough of every one of them. He'd never met anyone like Ada Carr in his life, and he knew now how empty all those days he'd passed before her had been. He hadn't lived an easy life. It had been fuller in some ways than others, but in this moment, Alonzo could only think of all those days before as lacking. Ada made everything else dim in comparison.

He took a step forward and then another, his breath slow and shallow, his pulse a pounding bass line. But every step was easier than the last because every step brought him closer to her. When he was close enough to hear the slightly dry wheeze of Ada's breath but not close enough to press his body against hers, he stopped.

Her mouth wilted into the prettiest petulant pout.

"That enough moves for you?" he breathed.

She tilted her head back, raised her nose and chin into the air in challenge. "No," she said before he could even fully ask the question.

Alonzo moved his hands slowly, giving them both enough time to anticipate what was coming. The spark of electricity when his fingertips landed on her waist. When he squeezed her flesh, they both shuddered.

And then there was the melody of her moaning sigh.

The bass of his gulping swallow.

Their hitched breaths as he gripped her and pulled her the rest of the way to him. She pressed, and he pulled, and when her body crushed against his, it was like a needle scratching the world. Everything around them came to a gaping, silent stillness.

"Are you always this careful?" she breathed against his chin, tilting her head back in invitation.

"You got a problem with that?" He whispered the question against her top lip, dry skin catching on dry skin.

She licked her lips. Their lips. "A bit, but I can work around that. Just need to know what I'm in for."

Alonzo shook his head. Their mouths brushed together. "I don't even know what I'm in for," he said and then pressed his mouth to Ada's. He swiped his tongue across the seam of her lips.

Her mouth opened on a breathy laugh. "Good. You seem like the kind of man who needs to be shaken up every now and then." She breathed those words into his mouth.

He tilted his head back and smiled.

She frowned.

"Is that what you're gonna do, Ada? Shake me up?"

She cupped the back of his head and pulled his mouth back to hers. "Haven't I already?"

He answered by kissing her again, and this kiss was better than the last. This kiss was art. It was a second encore in a hot, sweaty club where every note made your pulse quicken and took you to a new plane.

As far as Alonzo was concerned, kissing Ada Carr was like hearing a song for the first time and knowing it would change his life because she already had.

1967

ALONZO never usually drove in complete silence. He was the kind of person who tuned the dial to his favorite station and turned the volume up until his baseboards were shaking while he tapped out the beat of every song on the wheel. Every trip had a mood, and every mood had a soundtrack.

But not this trip. He followed Ada back to her motel with the radio turned off, his hands strangling the steering wheel and every muscle from his fingers to his toes coiled tight. His eyes were intent on the rear lights of Ada's car. He had to remind himself to breathe.

He needed the silence to convince himself that this was really about to happen.

Back at her motel, Alonzo pulled his car into the parking spot next to Ada. He turned the key in his ignition, took a deep breath, and then looked through his window to find her looking forward as if she too couldn't believe that this thing was real. But once his eyes settled on her profile, she turned her head to look his way.

He wondered if she could feel him watching her the way he could feel her eyes on him.

He hoped she could. He wanted that, he realized. He wanted Ada to know what she did to him, how much he wanted her because Alonzo had never wanted anything or anyone as much as he wanted Ada. He couldn't describe it, but sometimes feelings defied words.

For the last five years, nearly all of Alonzo's focus had been on surviving. Besides writing for the *Voice* and a few other local newspapers, he was always hustling. He did some handyman work in his neighborhood and ran errands for some of his elderly neighbors, and every now and then, when money was really tight, he picked up shifts making cabinets at a factory in Richmond. Both of Alonzo's parents were long gone, and even when they'd been alive, he hadn't had a soft place to land. Besides Toonie, who was hustling almost as hard, Alonzo didn't have anything like security or family. All he had was work, and he filled his life with it. For as long as he could remember, Alonzo had known that the only thing he could count on was what he could produce with his own two hands.

Even though he had dreams of writing full-time, reality took precedence. Bills were due today, the money in his pockets only stretched so far, and there was no one to catch Alonzo when he fell because everyone he knew was falling too.

But now there was Ada, and suddenly, all Alonzo could think about was a future he hadn't thought possible. A future where maybe he wasn't always falling, or maybe if he was, she was holding his hand as the bottom fell out from under them. And maybe they crawled back out of rock bottom together. It seemed naïve and embarrassing to want something that made him even more vulnerable than he already was, but he did.

So he calmed his breathing and waited to follow Ada's lead. When she pushed her door open, so did he. He mirrored her steps from the parking lot to the stairs.

The night was not quiet. He could hear cars on the highway nearby. Someone was singing "Break On Through" at the top of their lungs from...somewhere. A dog was barking somewhere else. There was nothing but racket, and while Alonzo heard those things, none of them stuck in his mind. There was only the way Ada's skin and hair seemed to drink up the harsh exterior lights on the building, transforming them into something so beautiful it hurt, the way her earrings brushed her bare shoulders as she walked, her delicate ankles as she bounced up the stairs, the backs of her knees, the curve of her ass, and then the flash of her grin as she looked over her shoulder and down her body at him. There was a damn good chance that he would dream about that smile for the rest of his life.

"You never did answer my question," he said, hustling up the stairs.

"Which one?" she laughed. "I swear you've been doing nothing but interrogating me all day. Like the article you're writing is about me."

Alonzo's stomach clenched at the unintended accuracy of her accusation. "So, are you saying you've been avoiding my questions on purpose? Or was that an accident?"

She turned around and began to walk backward with a wide smile on her face.

He loved the way she did that as if she needed to see him to keep their conversation alive, but also as if she trusted him to keep her from running into anything. And maybe even that she thought he would catch her if she fell.

He would.

"I don't believe in accidents," she laughed. "I think everything happens for a reason."

"So, you've been avoiding my questions because...?"

Ada shrugged. "'Cause I want to. 'Cause I can. 'Cause you let me."

Alonzo swallowed the lump in his throat. "You think me and you meeting was meant to happen?"

She rolled her eyes. "Course it was. But don't get too cocky. Just 'cause it's supposed to happen don't mean much. Even the temporary is necessary."

She stopped at her door and took her backpack off to get to her room key.

Alonzo took two quick steps, grabbed her around the waist, and spun her around again.

She gasped out a breath of laughter, and he pressed her back against the door. She spread her legs for him without hesitation.

He shifted his hips forward, nestling against her as that tingling feeling of something important washed over him again. Although now he knew that the 'something' he'd felt earlier wasn't about this damn festival or the story.

It was always Ada.

He held her gaze for a few heated seconds. "I asked if you had a man," he said, clarifying the important question she'd been dodging all day.

"Did you?

His fingers flexed around her hips. "You know I did."

Her hands moved up his arms slowly, heavily, as a wicked smile spread across her lips. "Well, I only answer that question to someone interested in filling the position." She panted out each word.

Alonzo's hands moved around her body to cup her ass, squeezing the soft flesh and pulling the sexiest moan from her lips. "I'm interested."

Ada groaned and wrapped her arms around his neck. She ground her hips forward against the growing bulge in his pants. "I can feel that."

Alonzo's eyes closed as he moved his hips against her. His mouth fell open on a groan, and he felt Ada's smile against his lips. "I don't have time for men," she whispered into his mouth, her tongue skating over his lips with every other word. "At least that's what my last few men would tell you."

Alonzo opened his eyes. He was surprised at how those words both excited and saddened him all at once. "I haven't had time for a girlfriend either," he said. "I don't even have a former lady to tell you that."

"I guess we're on the same page then."

He shook his head lightly. "I think I could make time, though. For the right person."

"Now why would you wanna go and do that? I told you, you need to be about your business—"

Alonzo lifted Ada up his body by the grip on her ass.

She yelped and wrapped her legs around his waist, tightening her grip on his shoulders. The smile was back on her mouth.

"Calm down, Ada Carr. I ain't asking you to marry me or nothing, I'm just sayin'."

"Just saying what, Alonzo Reid?" He was not mistaken. She moaned his name.

"I think you're right," he said, tilting his head back to look her in the eyes and offer his mouth.

Her head dipped unconsciously closer before she could stop herself.

"Everything happens for a reason," he continued, "but we don't know the reason yet."

Her eyes searched his, hints of desire and confusion

and maybe even fear battling for dominance. He would have let her work those feelings out at her own pace, but the quiet moment between them was interrupted.

"Hey, man, what the hell?"

They turned to see a door on the other side of the platform opening, a plume of smoke billowing out into the night air. Some white boy in brown bellbottoms, unbuttoned and falling off his narrow hips, stumbled outside.

"I thought we were all riding on the same wavelength! My bad. I thought you'd be into it."

Someone threw a shirt and backpack out of the room after him.

"Can't we talk about this?"

Alonzo let Ada down and shielded her while she unlocked the door. They didn't want to be in the middle of whatever was going down over there.

Ada pushed into her room and pulled Alonzo inside behind her. He slid the chain into place, and they stood by the door listening as the man continued to yell into the room down the hall for a few minutes before finally heading toward the stairs to leave.

Alonzo moved the curtain aside just enough to look out into the night. He watched as the man stopped in the middle of the parking lot to button his pants and shove his shirt into his bag. He stood still for a little bit longer, and Alonzo's gut clenched. But then he saw an orange flame light up the night. The man took a hit of his joint before resuming his walk. He was heading toward the highway, probably to hitchhike back to the fairgrounds. Alonzo finally exhaled when the darkness ate his form.

"He gone?" Ada asked after Alonzo had been silent for too long.

Alonzo nodded and turned around. He choked on whatever words were lodged in his throat because there was Ada, standing in the middle of her motel room, naked as the day she was born.

"Good," she said. "Let's pick up where we left off, shall we?"

Alonzo nodded numbly, pulling his t-shirt quickly over his head.

1967

ADA SAUNTERED to the bathroom like she was walking on a bed of flowers, flaunting herself, not for him in particular but just because she could. Just because she knew how beautiful she was.

Compared to her, Alonzo was like a tall tornado. His shirt got stuck on his ears, and his pants and underwear were so desperately tangled around his ankles that he fell over sideways on the bed. It was the most embarrassingly sad sequence of events in his entire life, but at least Ada hadn't seen it.

She'd heard it, though. "You alright in there?" she laughed.

Alonzo shook his head and buried his face in the comforter. "Fuck," he breathed at first and then turned his head and raised his voice. "I'm fine."

She only giggled in return.

Maybe other men might have found that sound dick-wilting, but Alonzo did not. His penis had been tortured by Ada's mere presence all day, and the heavy weight against his left thigh twitched at the sound. He might have wallowed in his own self-pity if he wasn't so damn turned on.

He sat up quickly and extricated his legs from his clothes. He pushed his socks off and darted toward the bathroom. At the door, he was breathing heavy and trying to hide it. Unfortunately, all the air whooshed from his lungs and gave him away because he found Ada bent over the bathtub. The view was breathtaking.

"Goddamn," he hissed, the air catching on his dry lips in an accidental whistle.

A year ago, Toonie had set him up with his flavor of the week's younger sister, and that had been a disaster for many reasons, but mostly because she'd told him the moment they met that she didn't like surprises, and she'd prefer if he stayed on her left side since she looked better from that angle. Alonzo drank half a bottle of beer, pretended he'd forgotten about a job in Berkeley, and high-tailed it out of his own apartment, fast as he could. He'd told Toonie the next day that high-maintenance women weren't his bag.

But once again, that wasn't quite right.

Nothing about Ada was low-maintenance. In fact, the day had been exhausting with all the sun and walking around and talking to new people on top of trying and failing to keep up with Ada's sharp tongue. He should have been so tired that he could barely stand, let alone speak, but he was energized. Every time he thought he was on the road to getting a hold of her, she shifted away, and all he could do was chase.

Ada had a lack of self-consciousness that made her comfortable in her skin in a way Alonzo found alluring but impossible to imagine. This bathroom was too bright by far, and yet her brown skin looked smooth and luminescent. She had a small scar on her hip and other dark nicks on her legs and back. There were light stretch marks over her hips and down the backs of her thighs. Her breasts were a small handful that lifted up into darker brown tips. Ada's body made his stomach rumble in literal hunger, and of course, she read his expression like an open book.

"You better be careful," she said. "I might think you want to eat me up if you keep looking at me like that."

"Would that be such a bad thing?"

"Look at you," she breathed.

"No," he said, blatantly moving his gaze from her face, down her body. "Look. At. You." He stepped into the bathroom carefully, his dick bouncing noticeably in front of him. If he hadn't been so enraptured by her, he might have been embarrassed about that, but he wasn't. There wasn't room for any kind of fear in this moment. "I love looking at you, Ada. Can't get enough of it. You."

"Love is a strong word," she said in a hushed whisper.

He stopped right in front of her and lifted a hand to

brush his palm just over the soft halo of her hair. Alonzo thought of so many ways he might respond to her, but he held himself back. He wanted to be careful with Ada and not just physically. So, he changed the subject.

In a way.

He bent forward to press his forehead against hers. "Is that what you want?" he asked.

"I—"

"For me to eat you up, I mean," he said, mimicking the smug smirk she'd been giving him all damn day.

She sighed a small, wheezing breath. "Yes."

He turned his head and brushed his mouth across her cheek. His lips caressed her ear. "Then let's get down to business."

Some moments in life are indelible. They don't just stick around in your memory; they become a part of you — they become necessary in explaining how you have become who you have become.

For Alonzo, there was the first day of second grade when he met Toonie.

The day his father left for good.

The day he *realized* that his father had left for good.

The first time he heard "A Change Is Gonna Come" on the radio.

When he heard the news on the radio that Sam Cooke was dead.

The past day had been full of so many moments that he couldn't imagine weren't already written into the fabric of his being. Ada's smile in the sunlight. Ada's laughter rising over the vibrato of Janis Joplin's voice. Ada's mouth touching his, the smoke drifting between their lips.

Ada bending over the sink as he sank to the cold tile floor behind her. The softness of her hips under his palms. The taste of her.

The soft hiss of her breath as it became a louder moan.

"Oh my God," she screamed when his lips covered the small bud at the apex of her sex. Those three words got louder and came together faster and faster until they were a melodic chant, encouraging him on.

He used his tongue on her in every way he could imagine, slipping inside of her as far as he could go to taste her hidden depths and then just using the tip to tease that bundle of nerves. He let her grind back onto his mouth and come apart on his tongue, and when her legs began to shake with the power of her orgasm, he wrapped his arms around her thighs to hold her up.

Some men might have felt powerful while breaking a woman like Ada down into a babbling mess, but if there was a power imbalance in the moment, everything he had, he gave to Ada.

It was already hers anyway.

ALONZO WIPED his mouth as he stood and smoothed his other hand up her back. "You gonna be alright here for a bit?" he asked.

"Don't let it go to your head," she rasped, the sting of those words undercut by her fast, wheezing breaths.

"Shouldn't you want to wait until you catch your breath to give me a hard time?"

Her smile was tired but happy. "You miss too many opportunities being cautious," she said. He liked that and committed it to memory.

He committed Ada to memory.

He squeezed her hip and moved to the tub to turn on the shower. He tested the temperature of the water and then turned back to Ada. She'd straightened up but was still leaning heavily on the counter.

She looked at him over her shoulder and grinned. "I bet you're the kind of man who didn't bring any rubbers?"

Alonzo started to cross his arms over his chest but stopped. He didn't know what to do with his limbs while standing butt naked and hard in front of her. "Wouldn't it be a turn-off if I came here with a suitcase full of rubbers but no place to lay my head?"

"Oh, honey, you are one of a kind," she teased. "There's a few in the makeup bag by my bed. I'd get 'em, but my legs aren't working just yet."

He grinned at her. "So *you* came prepared?" he teased.

"I am always prepared," she replied with a haughty sniff. "Well...usually."

He squinted at her, trying to understand what she'd meant by that, but she shooed him away. "Boy, stop thinking and go. 'Cause as soon as I can stand up on my own..."

She didn't need to finish the rest of that sentence. He was already sprinting back into the room.

When he returned to the bathroom, he reached for Ada, but she pushed his hands away. "Put it on."

He rolled his eyes. "I'm not tryna get you pregnant, woman."

"Didn't say you were," she said. "I told you to put it on. I wanna see." There was heat in her eyes as she said those words, and it sent a shiver down his spine.

How the hell did she do that to him?

He tore open the foil wrapper with shaking hands. Her gaze followed his hand down to his dick. She licked her lips as he wrapped a fist around himself and gave it a single hard tug. Her attention never wavered as he placed the condom at the head and began to roll it down.

"Slower," she rasped, reaching up to pinch her nipples.

"Jesus, Ada."

She smiled. "Jesus'll understand, I'm sure."

He sheathed himself in the condom for her. "Has anyone ever told you that you're dangerous?"

She lifted her head to look him in the eye. Her own gaze was hooded, and her chest was heaving with excitement. "It's possible," she said. "But you're the first man to ever make me feel just a teaspoon of regret."

Alonzo shook his head. "Don't. I just want to make sure you understand how damn bad you are."

She laughed and rolled her nipples between her fingers again. "Oh, I know. But I don't mind the reminder every now and again." She pushed from the wall and walked toward him. Her steps were shaky but careful. Her hand brushed over the length of him, and he groaned. Alonzo's thighs clenched, and his back bowed as he followed Ada to the shower on legs that might fail him before the night was over.

⸻

ANOTHER COLLECTION of moments Alonzo knew would define him unfolded like the petals of Ada's sex as he pushed inside of her.

The warmth of her pussy.

The specific key of her moans.

The soft bite of her fingernails into his back.

The strength of her thighs around his waist.

His name on her tongue as it pressed into his mouth.

The surety of knowing that this would be the first time but not the last.

"I think you're trying to prove a point," Ada sighed, "but I'm not mad about it."

Alonzo sucked her hard nipple into his mouth with a satisfied smile.

She tightened her legs around him and ripped a groan from his throat. Even without words, he knew what she was trying to communicate. She wanted him to move faster, and he would eventually, but not yet.

He wanted to savor every touch, every taste, every bit of joy and pain. So, he was moving as slowly as he could bear, his strength shored up by the skin of his teeth. He wanted to pound into her after an entire day of nothing but barely suppressed desire, the pressure of his own need building by the hour. But he wasn't in a rush for this to be over. He would never want to rush through a single second with her.

If he could spend his entire life inside Ada, it still wouldn't be enough.

So he made sure that this was a moment that would become part of her fabric, just as well as his. He dug his fingers into Ada's ass and lifted her against him. He licked a path up her chest and neck. His mouth met her ear, and hers met his. The sound of the water faded, and all he could hear was her keening moans.

"Ada?"

"Fuck," was her reply.

He smiled against her skin and thrust hard inside her before pulling out slowly. "Ada?"

"Oh God, what? There. Fuck. There."

Alonzo wrapped an arm around her waist and tilted her ass forward with his other hand.

She shivered and kicked her left leg out as he slipped deeper than he'd managed before. Curtain rings scraped the metal rod as the shower curtain disappeared and the light from the bathroom flooded into the dark shower. Alonzo nudged Ada's head to the left with his mouth. He licked the crown of her ear and then turned to see their reflection in the mirror.

"You still think I'm a square, Ada?"

She groaned and clutched him tighter. "Yes."

Alonzo watched his own muscles flex as he moved inside of her, the beautiful brown of her skin melding with his, matching images of shock and pleasure on their faces.

He watched her face as she spoke. "Maybe what I've been trying to get you to understand is that I *like* you just as you are. Maybe I more than like you just as you are."

Alonzo's back bowed as pleasure flooded his veins.

Ada might have said 'maybe,' but he heard 'definitely.' And as she fell apart around him, dragging him into his own release with nails scraping into the skin across his shoulders, Alonzo felt forever.

It would probably take Ada a while to catch up, but he was a patient man.

She'd figure that out eventually.

2010

"DADDY, do I really have to take these dolls?" Amaya asked, rushing into the dining room with a frown on her face.

Amir descended the steps behind her, the box of offensive toys in his hands.

Now that the last two bedrooms were packed up except for the big furniture, he'd started taping the boxes closed and hauling them into the foyer. He'd created neat stacks by the front door to make the move tomorrow easier. There was a small stack for Amaya that he was ready to start loading into her car just as soon as they handled the issue of these dolls.

Alonzo had moved a dining room chair into the living room after lunch so he could start packing up his records into the milk crates he'd sourced from Lord knew where. He started at the far end of the living room and began carefully plucking each album from the shelf. He wiped them down with a scrap of cloth and then lowered them into the crates. It had been a few hours, and when Amir walked into the living room, he was surprised to see how much progress his father had made. They still hadn't agreed on what to do with them, but whichever option they chose, they'd have to be packed up, so the sight made the tension in his shoulders ease a bit.

"I told Amir to tell you to keep 'em for now," Alonzo said.

"But they're creepy," his sister whined.

"I always told your mama you hated them things," Alonzo said, chuckling softly. He leaned over to place an album into the crate at his feet.

"I didn't *hate* them," Amaya said softly, chastened by Alonzo mentioning their mom.

Amir rolled his eyes, and then he coughed out the word 'liar.'

Amaya turned to glare at him over her shoulder.

Alonzo's chuckles turned to a full-blown laugh. "I might still got this baby face, but I sure 'nough wasn't born yesterday. You hate those things, and that's your right. Put 'em in storage," he said, looking up at Amaya. "You can hide 'em away if you want. But your mother was so damn happy to spend too much money on those dolls for you. All I ask is that you keep 'em while I'm here on this earth. I wanna be able to tell your mother that you held onto those God-awful things with a straight face when I see her again. You can get rid of 'em once I'm cold in the ground, okay?"

"Dad." Amaya's voice was wet with emotion.

Amir moved into the room as quietly as he could.

Alonzo leaned forward and plucked that last album from the shelf. "We shoulda kept the record player here just a little bit longer. Your mama used to play this album out. Hell, this might be a replacement for all I know."

"What album?" Amir asked.

He moved behind Amaya and placed a hand on her shoulder. Her muscles were tight, probably because she was trying not to cry. She hung her head forward, using her braids to hide her face. Amir squeezed her shoulder, and Alonzo reached out to grab her hand.

He answered Amir's question with a smile on his face. "Only man I ever worried your mama might actually leave me for," he said with far too much heat, considering both parties were dead.

"Teddy Pendergrass," he and Amaya said in unison with twin exasperated groans.

They knew this grudge very well.

1967

"CAN YOU SING?" Ada asked.

They were reclining on the bed, nearly naked, Marvin Gaye on the radio. They'd ordered a pizza from the only place open at this time of night and willing to deliver to their motel. Alonzo had thrown on a clean pair of pants to run down to the lobby. He bought a few cans of soda, and they stripped down to their underwear to eat a very late dinner.

It wasn't a date, but if it had been, this would have been the best date of Alonzo's life.

"Can I sing?" he echoed in a questioning whisper, thinking about it. Avoiding the question.

"I'll take that as a no," she laughed.

He scratched at his chin and laughed. "I don't even sing in the shower, I'm that bad."

She doubled over in laughter. "Damn shame."

"Is it?"

"Mmmhmm. I love a man who can croon."

"Croon?" Alonzo asked. He turned onto his side and leaned on one elbow, looking up toward the head of the bed.

It was a dangerous move, he thought, to look at Ada in nothing but a pair of panties. All that soft, bare skin, her nipples hard and calling to him, her body smelling like fresh peaches once more. The bedside lamp made a halo of her afro. Never mind. There was no danger, only certainty, he realized, as his dick started to harden all over again.

But he didn't look away.

Ada scooted down toward him, reclining on her side to face him. She paused for a second to let him look at her — and to look at him — before moving closer. They were so damn close that he could feel the heat of her surrounding him. She bent her leg, and her knee grazed the tip of his dick.

Alonzo swallowed a groan.

She reached out and dragged the tips of her nails through his chest hair. "I want a man who'll sing to me on our wedding day," she whispered.

"How you gon' get married if you don't want to date?"

"Don't get caught up on the details. I want a brotha," she continued, her nails moving down his ribs and stomach, "who's gonna memorize my favorite song and hum it for me when I'm sad." Her palm flattened against his lower stomach. His dick was practically jumping, trying to get closer to her hand.

Ada didn't move any faster. It was torture, but he'd endure it.

Alonzo lifted his own hand to stroke her cheek with his thumb. Ada closed her eyes and sucked her bottom lip into her mouth as her fingers slipped into his underwear.

"That's not asking for much," he said in a strangled whisper. "Not enough if you ask me."

"You think so?" Her hand circled the length of his shaft, and she began to stroke him in a loose, teasing grip.

His thumb moved toward her mouth, and her lips parted for him.

"I think when you meet the right man, he should give you everything you want just as soon as you ask, maybe even before."

She opened her eyes. "What if he can't sing? Should I ask him to learn?"

Alonzo's mouth curved into a smile, a soft moan escaping from his mouth. He pressed his thumb against her bottom lip. "I bet he'd try."

"Hmm." She pressed her lips together around his digit. He felt the tip of her tongue against his nail. She tightened her grip around him and stroked him harder. Faster.

"Goddamn," he breathed.

Ada began to suckle his finger as she scooted closer. She pushed him onto his back and used her free hand to pull his underwear down his hips just enough to free his dick so she could stroke him easily.

"Fuck," he sighed, closing his eyes, trying to breathe through this moment, so he didn't embarrass himself and come too soon.

She sucked intently on his finger once more before pushing his hand aside. Ada threw her leg over his lap with a sigh. She hovered above him with a hungry smile on her face.

When he looked between their bodies, he saw one of her delicate hands still cradling his shaft and the other pulling her underwear aside. She aimed the wet tip of his dick toward the warm cleft between her legs. He groaned and held his breath, waiting for her to sink down his length, but she didn't. Of course, she didn't. That would be too easy, and if there was one thing he was learning about Ada, it was that easy was not the name of her game.

But worth it absolutely was.

He fisted the blanket with one hand and cupped her breast roughly with the other. He didn't trust himself to hold her waist for fear he'd try to take over, but he couldn't help but touch her. He *needed* to touch her.

His thumb brushed her nipple as she moved his dick over her clit. She groaned. He shimmied up the bed, moving his dick through her folds. They groaned together at that contact and then focused, moving together to glide against one another.

"I read the obituary you wrote about Sam Cooke," she said out of nowhere.

Alonzo blinked, trying to follow the path of this conversation as it led from her pussy to that sad essay. He couldn't. "You did?"

She stroked the length of him and shifted her hips, rubbing herself up and down his length, but refused to let him inside. She was gorgeously maddening.

"H-how'd you find it?"

She shook her head. "Not today, but I thought I'd recognized your name when Ed told me you'd be filling in for Stu. I knew it was familiar, but I couldn't figure out where I heard it. And then today, I finally realized."

"Because you'd read my other piece." He was wet with her arousal and struggling to speak.

"I didn't just read that obit. I told everybody I knew to read it. I didn't know who you were, but I knew then that you were gonna be the next best music critic. One of us to write about us."

Alonzo was still blinking in confusion, some mixture of awe, embarrassment, and pride warring in his chest even as lust stripped him down to the bone. "Why are you telling me this now?" he asked, rolling her nipple between his fingers.

A small moan fell from her lips. "I think you're soft."

"Soft isn't really the word I'd use in this moment," he quipped, mostly to hide the sting he felt from that rebuke.

Ada pushed his hand from her breast and leaned

toward the bedside table. One of her nipples brushed his lips, and he licked it with the flat of his tongue. Her hand tightened around him again. She sat up straight, and he strained to keep his mouth on her for as long as possible. But then he was pressing his head back into the mattress because if it had felt good for her to watch him put on a condom, it was even better to have her do it herself.

"My goodness," he groaned.

Ada lifted from his thighs and finally — dear Lord in heaven, finally — began to lower her hips and let him inside her again.

He struggled to keep his eyes open to watch her, but he was thoroughly excited by the view.

Her breath was labored when she spoke again. "When I first read that obituary, I remember thinking, here was a man who's in touch with himself. He couldn't be real. But now I've met you, and I'll be damned if you ain't exactly what I thought you were. You're too damn nice, too damn nervous, and so damn soft."

Again, Alonzo wanted her to clarify what she meant because he felt harder than ever now that she was shifting her hips, riding him in slow, torturous circles. He couldn't concentrate on the song on the radio, but vaguely, he realized that she was moving in time with the beat, and that made him fall for her just a little bit more.

"I'm not soft," he ground out, fingers sinking into the blanket again.

She leaned forward, pressing her chest to his and

bracing herself on the mattress as she started to ride him faster and harder. "What I'm saying, Alonzo Reid, is maybe you have gifts that are more important than singing, but you're too damn nice to realize it."

"You think?" he asked, lifting his hips, desperate to feel the warm friction of her.

"It's a possibility," she gasped, grinding down onto him. "So what else are you good at?" Her eyes fluttered closed for a second, and she groaned a sigh.

"Let me show you," he whispered against her lips, and he licked at her smile.

Finally, he grabbed her about the waist and lifted her up his body until her wet sex was covering his mouth.

"Oh my God," she groaned as his tongue parted her lips.

She smashed one hand into his small afro, gripping his hair tight to keep his mouth exactly where it was. As if he had any plans to leave.

Ada's thighs clenched together, covering his ears. For a man who loved music and sound, the new kind of racket that came between Ada's thighs was something like a revelation. There was no quiet. There was his own pulse, her filtered screams. He watched her enjoy the pleasure she took from him. He tasted her in unhurried swipes followed by soft and then hard suction. Wherever he could get his lips and tongue, he licked and suckled and devoured. When she shivered, he sucked harder. When she cried out to Jesus, he angled his chin to rub her somewhere new. He dug his hands into the soft flesh of her hips. And when she came, wet and cursing and hissing and over and over again, his name was on Ada's tongue, just like her taste was on his.

———

ALONZO NEVER LEARNED to sing on key, but over the next thirty-eight years, every time Ada was sad, he put on some Teddy Pendergrass and buried his face between her legs.

Anything to make her shudder and smile and come like she had the weekend they met.

2010

"THIS IS MY JAM," Amir said, twirling a laughing Amaya in a circle in the middle of their living room.

Alonzo blinked at them in confusion for a second, but Amir pretended not to notice.

His father had told Amir once that after Ada died, he often struggled to keep his mind here in the present.

"Every day without your mama is dimmer than I can describe," he'd said once in an accidental, painful admission. "If given the choice, I'd happily go back in time to any day I spent with Ada."

Often, he returned to their first real date, he'd said. Amir knew that story by heart, he'd heard it enough times.

"I showed up at her house an hour late because my car broke down on 880. She opened the front door to the house she shared with your aunts Baby and Butterfly with a scowl on her face. It was a beautiful scowl, though. I just kept on *talking, explaining myself every which way until she agreed to walk down the street with me. We went to Foster's Freeze for burgers and ice cream."*

Sometimes he remembered when she was pregnant with Amaya. *"The only thing that could settle her or the baby was a very specific brand of Louisiana hot links. I spent three months driving all around the Bay to find them. But Lord, the smile she used to give me after that first bite was better than every best day I had before I met her."*

All these stories culminated in heartbreak. *"Some days, I wake up in bed alone and think of all the things I'd give up to go back to the days we spent around Lake Merritt with you two. Any day I woke up in bed with her."*

Amir hadn't known what to do with any of those stories. Words were Alonzo's trade, and the visceral descriptions of his grief were sometimes too much to handle. Even worse were the days when Alonzo didn't have the words to describe the cavernous depth of his loss.

But there was music.

Amir got it now, why his father was telling him this story as slowly and in as much detail as he could. But Alonzo was right; there wasn't any reason to hurry love. And there was sure as hell no rushing grief.

So he did the hustle with his older sister while their father watched with sad, damp eyes and that ever-present smile on his face.

2010

"THAT EVERYTHING?" Amir asked and then quickly clarified based on the question he could already see forming on Alonzo's mouth. "Everything you need for tonight?"

Alonzo smiled and nodded.

It was actually a ridiculous question to ask since they'd been moving Alonzo into Amir's condo for a couple of months. They'd gotten Alonzo a new bed since they were donating the old frame to a young couple in the neighborhood who'd been sleeping on mattresses on the floor. After the bed was in place, they started moving the rest of Alonzo's stuff in, piece by piece; some bookshelves that Amir had filled, organizing them by mood, the way he knew Alonzo would like, his typewriter on a spare desk in Amir's office, and his record player placed right in the center of his dresser.

They'd even done a few test runs. For the past few months, Alonzo had spent the night at Amir's here and there to let him get the feel of sleeping elsewhere. But this night wasn't a test run. Alonzo was leaving the house he and Ada had scrimped and saved and hustled to buy for good. He'd never sleep here again. He'd never make coffee in the kitchen that somehow always smelled of cinnamon, nutmeg, and vanilla. He'd never pull his grill out of the garage and dance to Earth, Wind & Fire with his wife in the backyard. The unspoken finality of this moment went unsaid, but they all felt it.

So, Amir asked as carefully as he could. "You got everything you need, dad?"

Alonzo was watching the house, looking at it the way Amir thought he might have the day after they got the keys — as if he couldn't believe that it was his. Theirs.

"There's a, uh…" He rested a palm on his forehead and closed his eyes to think. This was a familiar pose, so Amir and Amaya stood by and waited for him to find the perfect word to finish his sentence.

"There's a picture I haven't packed up yet," he said after a while. "It's in our room on that old dresser we're giving to, uh…" He snapped his fingers a few times.

"Kathy's niece Syrenity," Amaya offered helpfully.

Alonzo nodded. "Anyway, there's a bunch of framed photos on that dresser. Gon' get that for me, would you?" he asked, turning to Amaya, even though Amir had asked the question.

"I'll get it, pops," Amir offered.

"Nah," he said. "Maya, would you mind?"

"Sure, dad."

Amir watched as Amaya headed back into the house. "I could've gotten it, dad," he said once she'd disappeared inside.

"Let me do what I do, would you?"

"What's that mean?" Amir asked and then pressed his lips shut when Alonzo raised an eyebrow at him.

Alonzo walked to Amir's car and opened the passenger door. He crouched and sat down but kept his legs outside the door, feet planted firmly on the ground in his driveway. Not for the last time, but close to, sure enough.

Amir leaned against the side of his car and waited.

When Amaya returned, she had a small stack of picture frames clutched in her arms and pressed against her chest. She pulled the front door closed and checked to make sure that it was locked before walking back toward them. As she got closer, Amir realized that her eyes were wet.

"Maya?"

"I'm fine," she said, but she didn't look at him. She walked to their father and squatted in front of him, placing the frames on her thighs. "Daddy?"

There was a soft smile on Alonzo's face. "Your mama always meant to give you these pictures," he said. "I swear she spent months, hell, maybe even years, trying to find just the right frames for each one. When she..." He stopped abruptly and took a slow, deep breath. His eyes became glassy with tears, and he tried to blink them away as he looked at his daughter.

Amir looked away with wet eyes himself.

"When she passed, I found this stack of pictures in her studio. All of you. Your mama must've spent a small fortune on film when she was pregnant with you. If we could have afforded it, I think she would have taken a picture of herself every day she was pregnant with y'all. Actually, no, I *know* she would have done that." He was laughing gently when Amir turned around.

Amaya had balled her hand into her sleeve and was wiping at Alonzo's face.

He placed a hand on top of the frames, drawing their attention to the one on top. It was sepia-toned, a close shot of chubby baby Amaya in a pair of overalls and white t-shirt. "Most of 'em had frames, but for the ones that didn't, I took 'em down to Mr. Brewer. I picked this one out. I can remember the day she took this picture. You were supposed to be wearing this big white dress. It was bigger than your whole body. But just as soon as she sat you down on the living room floor, you spit up all over it."

Amaya was wiping at her own face now.

"She took you upstairs to change, and then you had a little...accident," he said with a smile.

"Dad," Amaya sighed.

"So then we had to give you a bath. And somehow,

these overalls were the only thing clean, even though this was not the look your mother wanted. But wouldn't you know it, as soon as she set you back down on the living room floor, you didn't spit up, you didn't fill your diaper, and you didn't cry. All you did was smile and laugh. She took this picture in one shot. She said you taught us a lesson that day, to just let you be you. That's what she wanted to capture. Every day she was pregnant, every outfit you ruined."

Amaya burst into a pained huff of laughter.

"Every day she spent being your mother, she wanted a picture to commemorate it. And when she was looking for all these frames, it wasn't 'cause she cared about the frames themselves but because she wanted you to hang them in your apartment and be swept away by the memories of how much she loved you." He cupped her face lovingly. "These were your mother's very favorite pictures of you, Amaya Kenya Reid. She wanted you to have these pictures so you would always remember yourself as she saw you: her baby, her twin, even though I did help a little. Perfect. From the moment you came screaming and howling into the world with those big doll eyes and head full of hair, your mama thought you were perfect."

There were rivers running down Amaya's face, and she squeaked each time she swallowed a small whining cry. But there was still a smile on her face.

"We thought the same thing of your brother," Alonzo added after a while, "even though his head was a little big."

Amaya's laughter sounded more like a pathetic howl of grief. Because it was. It was both.

Amir and Alonzo watched as Amaya clutched the picture frames to her chest, her body wracked with sobs. Alonzo brushed a soft hand over her hair, and Amir shielded his sister from as many prying eyes in the neighborhood as possible with his body, tears falling down their faces.

There was no rushing grief.

2010

ALONZO DIDN'T like Amir's condo in El Cerrito on principle.

It was new construction, and when Amir had first put his deposit down, his neighborhood wasn't anything more than a bit of turned soil, architect's plans, a few billboards announcing yet another housing development on questionable land too far from the closest BART station, and a dream.

Alonzo did not believe in suburban living. He'd raised his kids in the middle of the city where there was always something going on and where they were more likely to run into someone who knew their people than not. Amir and Amaya had been raised in a place where they had roots. They did not have roots in El Cerrito, and Alonzo hadn't ever let Amir forget it.

Amir felt guilty about moving Alonzo out of his

comfort zone, but Amir worked in El Cerrito, and his condo was smaller and more manageable for Alonzo as he aged. They'd talked about this as a family, but still...

"How'd you know?" Amir asked his father, just about halfway between Oakland and El Cerrito on I-80 East.

"Know what?" Alonzo was tapping his fingers against his knees. Parliament Funkadelic was on the radio.

"How'd you know Amaya needed those pictures? I mean, how'd you know when to give them to her?" Amir hazarded a glance toward his father and found him looking across the front seat at him.

"I didn't," he said matter-of-factly. "Your mama wanted her to have those pictures, and I finally remembered to give them to her. Simple as that."

Amir didn't turn toward his father because he didn't want to show the frustrated furrow of his brow.

But then Alonzo's left hand covered Amir's right on the steering wheel. "I'm not made of magic, son. And even though it pains me to say this, neither was your mother. We were just two people always trying to do right by you 'cause y'all didn't ask to be here, and we loved you."

Amir lifted his shoulder to wipe his wet face on it.

Alonzo continued. "Which isn't to say that y'all didn't get on our nerves sometimes. Every now and then, we had to go to the garage to smoke a little joint and relax."

"Oh my God," Amir groaned, laughing around each word.

"But we still loved you and never wanted you to think

we didn't. Your mama wanted Amaya to have those pictures, and I wanted to make sure she got 'em before you had to sort through all my stuff after I passed. She fretted about those damn frames," Alonzo said, the smile evident in his voice. "I kept telling her to just pick a frame or get a gift card or something. Let Maya pick out what she wanted. But you know your mama," he said.

Amir nodded slowly. "Art ain't about chance. Art is about that feeling in the pit of your stomach, that shakin' in your bones," he said, quoting his mother verbatim.

Alonzo's laughter was a gentle wheeze, soft and reedy. He patted his son's hand a few more times. "Art ain't nothing but love in the making," he added.

Amir felt strong enough to glance at Alonzo. "Didn't you used to say that music ain't nothing but making love on vinyl?"

There was a moment of silence as Amir changed lanes.

Alonzo laughed. "I used to say that to Toonie. Not you," he said, covering his mouth as he laughed. "You eavesdropping on me, 'Mir?"

Amir's laughter was so like his father's that they harmonized. "I might have once upon a time."

"Mmmhmm, I bet. But to answer your question, yeah. Music, photography, painting, books. We all take our own roads getting there, but hopefully, the destination is always love."

Alonzo fell silent. He was looking out of the passenger

window. Amir assumed he wasn't looking at the scenery since on this stretch of the highway, it was just rocky hillsides, with peeks of different small cities at each exit. Nothing Amir thought his father was interested in.

"The destination is always love," Amir said under his breath.

1967

None of us knows where the future is leading us. All we can do is hope.

In ten years, I hope to find myself at a barbecue. I want the smoke in the air to take me back to Monterey. I want to remember fire lighting up the stage, wild, sweaty flesh in a trance, peaches and cocoa butter on the air, the cacophony of instruments reminding me that life is nothing but chaos. Beautiful fucking chaos.

"The Monterey Pop Festival Was a Magical Weekend and Deserves to Be Remembered"
by Alonzo Reid
Staff Reporter
Village Voice, August 1967

ALONZO FELT ADA before he was fully awake. Before his eyes opened. Before his brain could fully process where he was or why.

He felt Ada's body wrapped around his side, her face pressed into the crook of his neck, her fingers scratching across his chest in sleep. Her soft breath tickling his skin. Her right leg wrapped around his.

Unlike Toonie, Alonzo didn't let his lady friends spend the night, but this morning, he guessed he could see the appeal after years of sleeping alone. But as with everything else, he accepted that the change in his opinion was as much about Ada as anything else.

"Lord, I can feel you thinking already," she whispered into his shoulder, kissing his skin.

Alonzo shivered and opened his eyes with a smile on his face. That had never happened before. When he opened his eyes, the motel room was light gray in the dawn. Ada's afro was flat on one side; her eyes were hooded. Her grin was sleepy and lopsided. If he'd thought she was beautiful last night, then there were no words to describe her this morning.

"I'm not thinking," he said.

Ada's laughter felt like heaven vibrating against the side of his neck. "I'm sure you meant to say something else. Let me know when you figure out what that is." She sat up and shifted on top of him.

Alonzo's face heated. "Hold on now," he said, trying to defend himself.

Unfortunately, Ada listened to him and froze, her body half-covering his, the tip of his dick resting just at the head of her mound, the warmth between her legs a teasing heat that made the muscles in his back spasm.

"I didn't mean it like that," Alonzo groaned.

"How'd you mean it, then?" She straddled his waist and leaned forward, her hands bracketing his head on the pillow, the wet lips of her pussy opening over his shaft.

"Holy shit, Ada," he hissed.

She giggled and shifted her hips, grinding her pussy up and down his shaft. "I bet your mind is running a mile a minute now."

Alonzo shook his head. "Not anymore. Surprised I can even string two words together."

"Let me work on that," she whispered.

The first kiss was on the center of his chest, the gentlest press of her mouth followed by another and another down his body. Those chaste kisses were somehow the most erotic touches of his life. She peppered a flurry of kisses across his lower stomach and scratched at his hips.

"You like this, don't you?" he ground out.

"Gonna have to be more specific than that." She said those words against his skin, her voice deep from sleep mixed with desire. She was pushing him slowly but insistently over the edge.

"You don't want a man, but you love making men fall in love with you." That was too many words, and he was panting as she pulled his underwear down his legs.

"Is that what you think is happening? I'm making you fall in love with me?" She whispered those words down his shaft.

Alonzo groaned loudly and scooted up the bed, and she looked up his body in amusement. "I want to see you," he said, shoving pillows between his back and the headboard.

Ada's tongue snaked up the length of him as she scooted forward.

"Yes," he groaned.

She sat up on her knees, leaning forward with her hands on Alonzo's legs. "No one's ever fallen in love with me because I know what to do between the sheets. Besides, men always think everything is love except love." She rolled her eyes and smiled.

Alonzo wanted to tease that word puzzle out, to ask for clarification, and to promise her that *he* wasn't like that, but he knew that was the wrong move. Trying to make promises neither of them knew if he could keep while her tongue was circling the head of his dick was exactly what she expected. So Alonzo didn't push Ada. He reached out and stroked his thumb across her cheek with a grin. "You like the attention, though," he said.

She turned her head and pressed a kiss against his palm. "What woman doesn't like attention?" She let go of him just long enough to pull off the shirt she'd thrown on sometime in the night.

Alonzo was mesmerized.

"I like when you watch me," she said. "Simple as that."

So he watched her as she laid on her stomach between his legs. He kept his eyes open while she grasped his dick in both hands.

There was a lazy grin on her face as she watched him back. Ada circled his dick with both hands and began to move up and down in slow strokes. She licked the head of his shaft in small explorations of his slit and then long swipes up and down his length. As his panting groans turned to loud moans, she moved one hand under her body to play with herself. And then she finally engulfed half of his dick in her mouth in one greedy pull.

They watched one another as Ada's mouth moved up and down his shaft. And he cursed her name.

They didn't look away when he told her he was close and then released into her mouth, although her eyelashes had fluttered closed for a brief second as she swallowed every drop.

When they recovered, she let him push her onto her back and make love to her slow and steady, the exact way he planned to love her for the rest of her life.

If she'd let him.

2010

"YOU SLEEP ALRIGHT, POPS?" Amir asked as soon as Alonzo came shuffling into the kitchen.

He was wearing a blue checked robe that he and Amaya had gotten him at least a decade ago, and he had a knit cap on his head.

"Your room wasn't cold, was it?"

Alonzo shook his head. "It was fine. Stop worrying. It'll take me a little bit to get used to being here, but you don't have to go running after me like I'm a baby."

Amir shoved his hands behind his back to hide the feeble clenching of his fists. He wanted to do something. He didn't like that there wasn't anything he could do to make this moment — and the next few days and weeks — easier on his dad. He hated feeling helpless.

Alonzo rubbed a hand over his gray beard. "But breakfast wouldn't be half bad." He lifted his eyebrows and nodded at a mixing bowl on the counter.

"Oh, yeah," Amir said. "I was gonna make you some flapjacks. Maya texted me mama's recipe."

Alonzo moved to the coffee machine and pulled a mug from the cabinet above it. "Then I'm gonna eat some flapjacks. I'll take a little bacon if you got it."

"Turkey bacon," Amir corrected.

Alonzo sighed as he poured his coffee. Before she died, Ada had transitioned her entire family from pork bacon to turkey because she'd read an article that said it was better for the heart and heart disease ran in Alonzo's family.

"I plan to be married to you for a long time, Alonzo Reid. So eat the damn turkey bacon," she'd said more times than Amir could remember. And of all the things he wanted to remember about Ada, it wasn't this. Because this memory hurt. It had always struck Amir as the height of irony and deeply unfair that Ada had switched to turkey bacon so she could enjoy as much time with her husband and children and then died just a few years later of a sudden unexplained heart attack. Even though he loved pork bacon and he ate it on occasion, when he'd been stocking the refrigerator for Alonzo, turkey bacon was the only option.

"Fine. Fine," Alonzo said. "But put it in the oven for a little bit at least. Let it try to get a little crispy."

Amir pulled the fridge open. "Try to get crispy?"

"We both know it ain't gone happen, but it's the thought that counts."

Amir laughed. "Alright, pops. Whatever you say."

———

THEY RETURNED to Oakland a lot less emotional than they'd left the day before. Thankfully, the soundtrack provided by KBLX seemed to fit their new mood.

"Aw yeah. Turn that up. Turn that up," Alonzo said when the deejay announced the next song.

Amir pursed his lips and squinted at his father in the passenger seat.

The older man was nodding along to the music, staring out of the window with a serene look on his face. His hands were free, though.

Maybe on a different day, Amir might have reminded his father that he had hands and could turn the music up himself. But the same filial urge that woke him up early to get Ada's flapjack recipe also gave Alonzo a reprieve. At least for today.

Amir turned his head back to the road in front of him and turned the dial so Alonzo could hear this song at the best volume to appreciate its genius. He sighed loudly before he did it, though.

If Alonzo heard him, he didn't respond, but he did start singing.

Baby, let's cruise

And Amir joined him because he hadn't grown up in the kind of household that could ignore a classic Smokey Robinson and the Miracles jam.

Awaaaaay from heeeere!

Alonzo turned toward his son and laughed as they harmonized together, or tried to, at least. The drive from El Cerrito to Oakland went by in a blip; Smokey, an extended Earth, Wind & Fire cut, and a disco medley that had Alonzo snapping his fingers and nodding his head in happiness.

It was a drive Amir wanted to remember, and he probably would; that soundtrack etched into the grooves of his heart.

1967

"LET me know if you see a shot you really want," Ada said as they walked back into the fairgrounds.

She'd told him the same thing yesterday, so he guessed that this was just her process.

He looked around the fairgrounds but had a hard time imagining immortalizing what he saw on film. After a day and a half, the grass in front of the stage looked a little worse for wear, and so did most of the concertgoers. They'd gotten enough pictures that Alonzo wasn't worried about the visual essay, but he didn't want to tell Ada that, just in case she saw something that moved her.

They squinted up at the stage. There were a few roadies setting up for the next act. Alonzo and Ada had missed the first few performances of the day making love. If he'd had his way, they'd have missed the entire final day of the festival, but Ada had dragged him back into the shower to get ready. Alonzo had tried his damnedest to change her mind, and he'd almost convinced her. She'd been whispering soft curses into his ear as he lifted her butt onto the bathroom counter when the housekeeper had knocked loudly on the door.

They'd rushed into their clothes, laughing and cursing and tripping over one another. Alonzo had helped Ada pack her bags to check out, and before he knew it, they were back at the festival. Stone-cold sober and in the cold light of day, the fair looked different to Alonzo, not nearly as beautiful as he'd thought last night.

"We could get another motel room," he whispered into Ada's ear.

"Hush," she said, shoving him with her shoulder. She looked at him out of the corner of her eye, an adorable smile playing at her lips.

He wanted a picture of that, he realized. That's what had changed. The festival was what it was, but Ada was the point of it all. "Lemme see your camera."

The camera in question was slung over her neck, nestled between her breasts, accentuating the hard points of her nipples — or maybe that was just where his attention seemed to drift naturally. Either way, she was a vision in a tank top and a pair of tight jean shorts that looked painted onto her legs.

"I don't let anyone touch my camera," she said in a clipped voice.

"What?"

"You heard me," she said. "No one touches my camera but me."

He crossed his arms over his chest and turned to her. "Do I need to remind you," he lowered his voice to a whisper here, "that I was nuts deep inside you barely an hour ago? My tongue has seen parts of you my eyes haven't."

Ada crossed her own arms over her chest, unfortunately covering those perfect nipples. "There's no need to whisper. A woman's pleasure is not taboo. And a man who knows how to use his tongue," her voice *rose* here, which made Alonzo's face heat even as the smile on his face widened. "That's not a thing to be ashamed of unless you're trying to convince me to do a thing I just *told you* I will not be doing."

"Ada."

"Alonzo?"

They stared at one another for a long, tense moment before he sighed and dropped his arms. "I just wanted to take a picture."

"Then you should have brought a camera."

"Of you," he said with a sigh and rolled eyes.

"What?"

"I just wanted to take a picture of *you*, Ada."

"Well, why the hell would you want to do that?"

Alonzo shook his head and turned back toward the stage. "Because."

"*Because* is not an answer. Did nobody ever tell you

that?" She grabbed his arm and turned him back around to face her.

He put his hands on his hips. "I think this might be *another* reason you don't have a man."

"Obviously," she scoffed. "Now explain yourself."

"You really don't get it."

"Get what?"

"You!" he yelled. "How in the world does a woman like you not get that you are it? You are amazing and beautiful and frustrating. From the minute we met, you've been giving me nothing but aggravation, but still, you're all I can think about. You are a pain in the ass, but I think I'd see red if you were out in the world being a pain in somebody else's ass, Ada. How do you *not* get that?"

Ada's hands had fallen down to hang limply at her side while Alonzo unloaded a shocking amount of emotion on her. Emotion that didn't make sense to his brain, considering how little time they'd known each other, but felt perfectly reasonable in his gut.

So he kept going. "I've barely known you two full days, but I sure as hell know that two damn days ain't enough. There's probably a whole bunch of brothas all over the East Bay — hell, why not the state. I bet there's a whole gang of men in every county in California wondering what you're doing right now. And maybe in a few months, I'll be the one in Alameda."

"You barely know me," she said with a halfhearted

shake of her head. She crossed her arms again, trying to look unaffected, but then dropped them immediately.

Alonzo wasn't done yet. Since he'd already started telling her too much, it seemed best to just keep going. "I know I don't know you, Ada. But I want to know you. I want to get to know you. That's what I can't believe you don't get. I can't believe you thought anyone could spend a few hours with you, let alone days, and not be completely enamored by you. You might not feel the same, and that's okay, but I wanted a picture of you right now, just in case. If this is the last day I ever see you, you're the kinda person I want to remember. You're *worth* remembering."

She blinked up at him, and if not for the small flare of her nostrils as she inhaled deeply, he might have thought she'd been completely unaffected by everything he'd said. But she wasn't.

"What makes you think you're gon' get rid of me that easily, Alonzo Reid?" she whispered fiercely.

Those few words in her husky voice blew him away. Alonzo was on cloud ten because cloud nine wasn't high enough.

As the crowd's rippling excitement steamed around them, he and Ada watched one another. "I didn't say I was trying to get rid of you."

"Sure sounded like it," she accused.

"Everything I said, and that's what you heard?" he asked.

"Yeah." Her smile made Alonzo's heart stutter. She

shrugged the camera strap over her head and turned it around in her hands. "Don't move," she commanded as she turned and then backed into him, molding her body against his. "I gotta get the angle right."

Alonzo wrapped his arm around her instinctually. "Nowhere to go. Nowhere else I'd rather be," he whispered into her peach and cocoa butter-scented neck.

2010

"REIDY. REIDY, WHERE YOU AT?"

"Clarence, if you don't lower your voice," Wanda said in an exasperated tone.

Amir was in the living room with Alonzo, tackling the record collection, the very last thing they needed to pack before the big move could begin.

"Negro, if you don't stop yelling in my house," Alonzo yelled.

"We're in the living room," Amir yelled.

"Boy, did you not just hear me?" Alonzo said before shaking his head and turning back to the records.

"We brought lunch," Wanda called, but Alonzo didn't tell her to lower her voice.

Amir stood as Wanda breezed into the room with a smile on her face.

"As-Salam Alaikum, Amiri," she said with a smile on her face.

"Wa-Alaikum-as-Salaam, auntie." Amir wrapped his arms around his aunt, and as Wanda so often did since Ada's death, she squeezed him just a little bit tighter than normal, her small arms surprisingly strong.

"Reidy, what's happening?" Toonie called from the kitchen. "We went by that Greek spot you like."

"What'd you get?" Alonzo asked.

"Oh, we got a little bit of everything. Whatever we don't eat, you two take home, okay? Then you won't have to cook for the next few days."

"I know how to cook, auntie."

Toonie scoffed from the kitchen.

Alonzo stood from his chair and dusted his hands off. "I'll have you know my boy made some flapjacks for me just this morning."

"Oh, yeah? Did you watch him do it?" Toonie teased.

Wanda patted Amir's chest and then let Alonzo give her a peck on the cheek on his way to the dining room. They followed behind him.

Amir pulled a seat out from the table for Wanda to sit and crowded into the small kitchen to wash his hands after Alonzo. They didn't have any more plates or silverware, but Toonie and Wanda had gotten paper plates and plastic silverware. They brought the platters of food to the table, which would be going to Toonie and Wanda's oldest son next week. He'd just moved into his own apartment after a divorce, and Alonzo was worried about him starting over on his own. A table wouldn't solve his problems, but at least he wouldn't be eating over the sink.

Alonzo sat in Ada's seat just as the front door opened.

"We're here," Amaya called from the front door.

Amir's butt barely kissed the chair before he jumped back up.

He rushed into the living room for the fold-out chairs while his elders scooted around the table to make room for Amaya and her girlfriend, T'Kaia.

"What y'all eating?" Amaya asked, moving around the table to give Alonzo, Wanda, and Toonie kisses on the cheek.

"Greek," Wanda said.

T'Kaia slapped hands with Toonie, hugged Wanda, and bumped fists with Alonzo while Amir slid the fold-out chairs into place. Everyone waited for Wanda and Toonie to pray before they dug into their food. They mostly ate in silence, and it struck Amir that he had never eaten a meal in this house in silence. There was always music playing or someone singing, he and Amaya arguing about something trivial, and if all else failed, there was the soundtrack of Alonzo whispering to Ada and then her shocked, loving laughter.

But maybe the silence was how they would say goodbye.

MOVING OUT WAS CHAOS.

Most of Alonzo's leftover items could fit in the car, but they'd rented a small truck to take the furniture they were giving away to friends and family members across town. Amaya and T'Kaia were packing up the last of her things, including that box of dolls, which she'd somehow forgotten to take yesterday. And the church had sent its own truck to collect last-minute donations.

There weren't any professional movers, just friends and family members and young boys working off a punishment helping them haul boxes and furniture out of the house. Amaya was making sure every box and piece of furniture made it into the right truck. Toonie and T'Kaia were making sure no one broke anything on the way out. Wanda was cutting up watermelon in the kitchen for a post-move snack. And that left Amir and Alonzo in the living room, finally ready to settle the matter of the vinyl records.

"I know we're taking them to my house, pops," Amir said, stacking the crates two on top of each other. They'd take what they could in Amir's car and store the rest at Toonie and Wanda's and even a few in Amaya's care for her to bring when she visited in a few days.

Alonzo was slowly emptying the very last shelf. "Good, but do you know why?"

Amir stood up straight with his hands on his hips. "Pops."

"Sounds like a no's 'bout to come out that mouth."

"Aren't I too old for this?"

"Never too old to learn a lesson."

"They absolutely tell parents to say sh— stuff like that, don't they? Like they give you a baby and a handbook of corny things you gotta say, right?"

Alonzo chuckled as he wiped down a Patti Labelle album Amir recognized but couldn't name off the top of his head, to his own chagrin. "I mighta read that in a pamphlet somewhere, maybe."

"Pops."

"Amir Malcolm Reid," he said, looking up at him.

"Was the whole name necessary?"

"You're stalling, so yes, it was."

Amir shook his head and looked around him. He took in all of these records that would fill his small living room to bursting soon enough. Just a few of these crates would probably weigh his car down enough that he'd pop a tire. These things were more trouble than they were worth, he thought, and then caught himself.

He tried to see them the way his father did. The way he had before figuring out how and where to store them was part of the calculation. It took a while for his brain to adjust, but when he did, all he could see — all he could hear — was Aretha and the smell of Pine-Sol first thing on a Saturday morning, Parliament Funkadelic that one time the kids were both on the honor roll at the same time, the Jackson 5 when they celebrated the end of a school year, the Gap Band on a random spring day when nothing more interesting was happening than the sun rising in the sky.

His parents had given him a soundtrack with these records. He'd learned how to wring every ounce of joy out of life with this music. His first break-up with a girl, he'd come straight home, found Billie Holiday singing the standards on vinyl, put it on the record player, and then dramatically laid on his back in the middle of the living room. And his parents had let him. When Amaya had complained that she wanted to hear something, anything, else, they'd quietly told her to let Amir work through his heartbreak. These albums were an extension of his parents' love. The lyrics were baked into Ada's photographs, and Alonzo's books were sentimental prayers to them. This music was threaded through all Amir's memories of his parents and this home.

One day, Alonzo would be gone, and Amir wouldn't be able to remember the exact pitch of his or Ada's voices. But he would still have the music, and it would almost be like having them back.

"They're the soundtrack you and mama made together," Amir said solemnly.

"That's my boy," Alonzo whispered back.

1967

"WHAT DID that guitar ever do to deserve this kinda disrespect?"

Ada's giggles and the sound of her camera capturing this moment were her only reply.

They'd gotten closer to the stage when the Jimi Hendrix Experiment came on, and thank goodness because Ed would have killed them if they hadn't gotten a series of pictures of the musician setting his guitar on fire. Even if seeing it in person made Alonzo sick to his stomach.

"He can replace the guitar," Ada teased.

"That's not the point."

She laughed again and turned her camera on the crowd. The sun was setting, and the lighting wasn't great, but he turned with Ada, happy enough to tear his eyes from the instrumental tragedy happening in front of him. Even without good lighting, he could see Ada's vision.

"What's the point then, Alonzo?"

He took a deep breath and let it out on a sigh.

"Oh Lord," she laughed.

Alonzo smiled in spite of himself. "How much you think that guitar cost?" he asked her.

"More money than either of us got."

"Exactly. So why burn it?"

She lowered her camera but continued staring out at the crowd, looking for another shot. She shrugged. "'Cause he can. 'Cause he wanted to."

"That's not a good enough explanation."

"Yeah, it is." She turned to him and let her camera go. Ada placed both hands on his shoulders and lifted onto the balls of her feet, so they were almost eye-to-eye.

Alonzo grabbed her around the waist and pulled her to him. She laughed and smiled, and he smiled back, the frustration he'd just felt beginning to seep out of his pores.

"Why do you like writing?" she asked.

"'Cause I like music. Love music," he corrected.

"And why do you love music?"

He swallowed painful flashes of memory and answered her with a husk in his voice. "'Cause it takes me away. It makes me feel free."

Ada wrapped her arms around his neck and stepped closer before turning her face toward the stage. He didn't look at the fire, but he saw the orange flames and stage lights playing across her skin. "The point of it all, his music and my pictures and your writing, is to find a way to get free. No one path is gon' be right for all of us."

Alonzo tightened his arms around Ada's waist and hauled her into them. "Maybe," he conceded.

"Possibly."

"If we're all heading toward freedom," he said, "then maybe some of us are heading down the same road in different shoes."

She bit back a smile and turned to him.

When she turned the full force of that smile on him, it was impossible for Alonzo to be all tied up in knots of anger. Not when he was so close to her, so he let it go. If Jimi Hendrix wanted to burn his guitar, then at least Alonzo had something good to write about in his story, and Ada had a damn good picture for the front page.

Sometimes life was as simple as that.

2010

"WE'RE ALMOST DONE," Alonzo said from his seat on the front porch.

Amir was huffing and puffing, covered in sweat. He stopped to wipe his face with his t-shirt and then finally took it off. "We?" he asked, looking at the crates of records currently piling up in his garage. "Are we almost done? 'Cause I'm certain I'm the only one hauling all these records."

Alonzo shrugged. "I'm here for moral support. Only a couple more crates left."

Amir couldn't help but laugh. What else was he gon' do besides shake his head and get back to work?

"Oh, hello, neighbor."

Amir turned to see who Alonzo was speaking to. He'd lived in this condo for two years, and he'd never spoken to any of his neighbors. Mostly that was because no one had lived in the condo next to him for the same amount of time. But he was also rarely here. He worked too much and spent most of his free time in Oakland with Alonzo or the city with Maya to get to know his neighbors.

But clearly, that had been a mistake.

"Hello," a woman he had never seen a day in his life replied to Alonzo. There was a confused smile on her face as if she wasn't used to chatting with the neighbors either.

"Just moving in?" Alonzo asked. His question made Amir take notice of the broken-down boxes in her hands.

"Um...yes, sir."

Alonzo waved a hand in the air. "Call me Alonzo. I'm just moving in too. This is my son's place." He gestured toward Amir, and her eyes turned to him and then widened.

"Oh," she breathed.

"Amir, come help this nice young lady with her boxes."

It took a few seconds for those words to sink in. When they did, Amir rushed forward, forgot the curb, and tripped. "Damn," he mumbled in embarrassment.

"Language," Alonzo warned.

"Pops, come on," Amir whined while his neighbor covered her mouth, trying to stifle her laughter and failing.

When he made it to the bottom step of her porch, he smiled, and her eyes widened again, darting from his face to his bare chest and back again.

"Hey...neighbor," Amir said. As soon as the words were out of his mouth, he wanted to punch himself.

"Hey."

"Um, my name's Amir, and that's my annoying father, Alonzo."

"I already said all that," Alonzo groaned.

She was still trying not to laugh at them or ogle him too openly. If Amir hadn't been so damn physically tired — and Alonzo hadn't been right there all in their business — he might have commented on that. He could not flirt with a girl in front of his father.

"My name's Imani," she said once she got herself together.

"Oh, that's a good name," Alonzo interjected.

"Beautiful," Amir said.

She was losing the battle to hide her smile, and the more he saw of it, the more he liked.

"Boy, if you don't take those doggone boxes from her," Alonzo ordered.

Imani lost it then. She laughed so hard she dropped her boxes.

Amir rolled his eyes and stooped down to pick them up for her. She crouched down, and they were eye-to-eye for the first time.

"I'm sorry." She was still laughing.

"Don't be. I know what he's like."

"I can hear you," Alonzo muttered.

Amir decided to ignore him. "When'd you move in? Ain't nobody been here for a while."

"This weekend. I didn't think anyone was in your place, either."

"Oh, yeah, I've been helping move dad out of his house in Oakland."

"Oh, is that where you're from?"

"Yeah, born and raised. What about you?"

"Virginia."

"You just moved here from Virginia?"

"Yeah. I, um, I got a job opportunity, and I couldn't pass it up," she said, stacking the last flat piece of cardboard onto the stack for him.

Amir made sure he could hold the stack securely before he stood and looked up at her. "What do you do?"

"I'm a violinist. I'm joining the Oakland Symphony."

"Oh," Amir breathed. "Wow."

Ada used to tell her children to follow their gut, that they could never go down the wrong road if they listened to their instincts. And instinct told Amir that Imani was something special.

"Well, thanks," she said after Amir had been staring at her for far too long in silence.

"Oh, yeah. Yeah. No problem. Recycling pick-up is on Tuesdays. I'll put 'em in my can if you don't—"

She shook her head. "I don't. I called the city before my move, and they told me they'd have a can here when I arrived, but they didn't."

Amir nodded. "That's not a shock. You'll probably have to call a couple more times."

She rolled her eyes and sighed. "I figured. Thanks again.

"If you have any other recycling, I'm just next door," he said. "I mean, until your can shows up, you're welcome to use mine."

Her eyes darted to his chest one more time. "Thanks, I'll probably take you up on that."

"Please do."

She smiled at him fully for a long moment, and then she turned to his dad. "Nice to meet you, Alonzo."

"Nice to meet you too, Imani. See you around."

Amir watched as Imani ducked back into her house, and maybe a few more seconds after that.

"Okay, boy, don't be weird," Alonzo said.

Amir sighed and turned to glare at his father. "You're one to talk."

"What? If it wasn't for me, you'd still be standing at the curb looking foolish."

"Pops."

"Amir," he laughed. "Put those boxes in the trash and get those last few crates into the garage. We can reheat something for dinner and watch a movie. And in a couple weeks, we'll call Toonie and have him bring his saw over. We'll start building a shelf for these records."

"Build? Pop, we can just buy some."

"The hell we can. You know how expensive those are?

Besides, we'll do it out here in the driveway. Maybe your new neighbor'll bring you some lemonade."

"Pop, keep your voice down," Amir hissed, dumping the boxes into his recycling can.

"For what? Look, listen to me when I tell you that when you meet a woman who might could be the one, you don't want to play it safe. You miss too many opportunities being cautious."

Amir shook his head as he headed back to his car.

"You laughing, but you gon' realize I'm right one of these days."

"Am I?" Amir laughed.

"Damn right."

"Language," Amir teased, and they both laughed as Amir unloaded the last of Alonzo's records in what seemed like the blink of an eye.

EPILOGUE
2019

"OKAY, put that album next to the other album," Amir said. He was sitting on the living room floor with a crate of records next to him. The first of too many.

"Daddy, what's a album?" Amani asked.

"We talked about this already," Amir said. "It plays music." He handed her another album, and she held it in her hands, looking at it in confusion.

"How?"

Amir sighed at the thought of going over this lecture for the third time. "How 'bout we finish unpacking this crate, and then we'll go to Rae's to pick up dinner. I'll tell you about how the albums play music then, okay?"

She squinted up at him with a mischievous smile on her face. "Can we get pie?" she whispered.

Amir laughed. "Yes. We can get pie."

His daughter hustled that album onto the shelf, and they settled into a groove.

This was their first night in the house where Amir had grown up, and he was trying to make sense of his feelings at being back here in this way. They'd rented the house out for a few years before Amaya and T'Kaia had been priced out of San Francisco. They'd lived here for nearly five years, and Amir had assumed that things would stay the same.

But then Amaya had been offered a job teaching fine arts in Toronto, and then Imani had gotten pregnant again after nearly four years trying for a second baby, and suddenly, they were shuffling homes again. Amir had just been here last month to help his sister's family move out, and now he was trying to get his family settled in. Life was chaos, and undercutting it all was a grief he knew he'd never escape.

He wondered what his parents would think of Amaya moving to another country. He wanted to ask his dad how they'd managed to raise two kids when some days, Amani was more work than he thought he could handle. He wanted Ada to meet Amani. He didn't want Amani to forget Alonzo.

"Do you remember whose albums these belong to, Mani?"

She shook her head. "Grandpa Zo," she said.

Amir held the next record back. "If you remembered, why did you shake your head?"

She reached for the record with a smile and then nodded her head. "I forgot."

He wasn't sure if she meant that she'd forgotten her grandfather or she'd forgotten how to nod. Each option was just as likely as the other, and there wasn't any point in grilling a five-year-old for a direct answer.

"Daddy grew up in this house," he told her.

"With auntie Maya?"

"Yep. And Grandpa Zo and Nana Ada."

She stopped at that last name and bit her bottom lip in childlike concentration. She looked like Maya when she did that. "I don't 'member Nana Ada?"

He swallowed a sob and blinked back tears. "No, sweetie. You never met her. But you met Grandpa Zo."

Her face lit up, and she nodded this time. "He was my best friend."

Amir nodded. Alonzo was the first person besides Amir and Imani to hold his daughter. Just like he was the first person to hold Amaya's son, his namesake. There were hundreds, maybe even thousands, of pictures of him with his grandchildren, who became the center of his life in his last few years. For a while, after Maya had Alonzo, they'd watched their father come back to life. For the first time in years, he'd been something like the man he'd been when Ada was alive.

But that bright flash of rejuvenation had lasted the first two years of Amani's life, and then he'd faded again.

It wasn't any easier to lose Alonzo. In some ways, it

was harder. Who would remind him of Ada's favorite sayings? Who would clap him on the shoulder and give him a good squeeze when he needed it? Who would laugh at his bad jokes with his entire body? Who would play him some deep cut and give him a lecture about that song's history, whether he wanted it or not? Who would love him the way Alonzo had? Who would know just the right song to play to capture the mood of an ordinary Wednesday evening?

No one.

Some days he woke up, and those holes in his soul where Ada, Alonzo, Toonie, Wanda, and Lena lived were angry screaming wounds. And some days, they were dull aches of acceptance. But no matter how he felt, he knew the best way to ease the pain of those losses was to love Amani harder — to give to her what Ada and Alonzo had given to him and remind her of where she was from.

He pulled his phone from his back pocket and saw he had a text from Imani. She was at practice and would be ready to go in about an hour. If they timed it right, they could unpack this last crate, call in an order at Mama Rae's, and pick it up after they got Imani. He texted his plans to his wife and then pulled up the Spotify app.

"Okay, Mani, what's the mood?" he asked, scrolling through his playlists.

He was prepared for her to ask for one of those God-awful children's playlists that he suffered through, wondering if his parents had done the same. He couldn't imagine Alonzo tainting his ears with Barney, but maybe they had. He had loved him more than enough to suffer through that.

Surprising him, Amani threw herself against him for a hug, knocking the air from his chest in the way only little kids who don't know the power of their little bodies could. "You pick, daddy," she said. "Just don't cry, okay?"

He wrapped his arms around her. The dome light on the ceiling glinted off his wedding band. Alonzo's wedding band. He held his daughter tight for a few seconds. "Okay, honey. I won't cry."

He turned her around to look at his phone as he scrolled to a playlist that was older than her with some songs older than him. Alonzo had created it for him years ago and then had painstakingly transferred it to Spotify, squinting at the computer screen, searching for the exact versions he needed.

Amir played this playlist regularly, in those moments when he needed to remember Alonzo as he lived, from one beat to the next, in the etched grooves of these albums and his son's heart.

"Oooh, I 'member this song," Amani sang, sounding exactly like Ada in her excitement.

"Do you?" Amir asked as the horn-heavy intro to a classic Earth, Wind & Fire song rang out from his phone.

She nodded and then started jumping around the living room, dancing in hops and jerky sways like most kids did. They were on a tight schedule, but Amir put the records aside and joined her, dancing around the living room just like he had when he was her age.

He couldn't think of a better way to return home.

Every time we hear a song, it's both old and brand-new. That's the point of music. Not the technical aspects, the precision of the musician, or even the lyrics. It's the way the music makes you feel when you're up, down, and running around in circles. It's the possibility that you can hold onto that feeling and nurture it. That you can build something new along the way.

That the song is only the beginning.

The Summer of Black Love: Music and the Making of a Revolution, Alonzo Reid

SELECT BIBLIOGRAPHY

Monterey Pop (1968)

Ida Mojadad, "They were the soul of the airwaves," Media Museum of Northern California

Gretchen Lemke-Santangelo, *Abiding Courage: African American Migrant Women and the East Bay Community*

ACKNOWLEDGMENTS

I have lots of ideas for stories, but they don't always turn into something I can read or share. When one of those stories does turn into ~something~ it's usually because I have really great people in my life who are willing to co-sign the half-formed ideas I cook up usually in the middle of the night. *Back in the Day* was no different. Thank you Kai for asking the important questions like, "Do these characters have faces?" and then riding with me through the chaos of my "schedule." Thanks Lucy, for pushing me to turn this idea into a thing. Thanks to the rest of LLC Twitter, Tasha and Zaida, for listening to my word count and tear updates and then sharing something terrible from Tik Tok probably. And thanks Amy Jo Cousins for accidentally helping me put the final piece of this puzzle into place very late into this story.

If you liked this *Back in the Day*, please tell a friend. And if you're so inclined, please consider leaving a review wherever you feel comfortable. And feel free to reach out to me on my socials or sign up for my newsletter.

OTHER BOOKS BY KATRINA JACKSON

Heist Holidays

Grand Theft N.Y.E.

The Family

Beautiful and Dirty

The Hitman

Bay Area Blues

Layover

Back in the Day

Standalone stories

Encore

Office Hours

The Tenant

Sex Toy Soldier

www.ingramcontent.com/pod-product-compliance
Lightning Source LLC
Chambersburg PA
CBHW071908220626
47052CB00002B/265